JAMES PATTERSON & CHRIS GRABENSTEIN

ILLUSTRATED BY KERASCOËT

JIMMY Patterson Books
LITTLE, BROWN AND COMPANY
NEW YORK BOSTON

Copyright © 2023 by James Patterson
Illustrations copyright © 2023 by Kerascoët

Excerpt from *Minerva Keen's Detective Club* copyright © 2023 by James Patterson

Cover art copyright © 2023 by Kerascoët. Cover design by Tracy Shaw. Cover copyright © 2023 by Hachette Book Group, Inc.

JIMMY Patterson Books / Little, Brown and Company
Hachette Book Group
1290 Avenue of the Americas, New York, NY 10104
JimmyPatterson.org

First Edition: March 2023

JIMMY Patterson Books is an imprint of Little, Brown and Company, a division of Hachette Book Group, Inc. The Little, Brown name and logo are trademarks of Hachette Book Group, Inc. The JIMMY Patterson Books® name and logo are trademarks of JBP Business, LLC.

The publisher is not responsible for websites (or their content) that are not owned by the publisher.

Little, Brown and Company books may be purchased in bulk for business, educational, or promotional use. For information, please contact your local bookseller or the Hachette Book Group Special Markets Department at special.markets@hbgusa.com.

Library of Congress Cataloging-in-Publication Data
Names: Patterson, James, author. | Grabenstein, Chris, author. | Kerascoët, illustrator.
Title: Jacky Ha-Ha gets the last laugh / James Patterson and Chris Grabenstein; illustrated by Kerascoët.
Description: First edition. | New York : JIMMY Patterson Books/Little, Brown and Company, 2023. | Series: Jacky Ha-Ha | Audience: Ages 8–12. | Summary: Twelve-year-old Jacky spends the last weeks of summer at theater camp with new friends, lots of jokes, and plenty of drama.
Identifiers: LCCN 2021048381 | ISBN 9780316410090 (hardcover) | ISBN 9780316410229 (ebook)
Subjects: CYAC: Camps—Fiction. | Theater—Fiction. | Humorous stories. | LCGFT: Humorous stories.
Classification: LCC PZ7.P27653 Jad 2023 | DDC [Fic]—dc23
LC record available at https://lccn.loc.gov/2021048381

ISBNs: 978-0-316-41009-0 (hardcover), 978-0-316-41022-9 (ebook)

Printed in the United States of America

LSC-C

Printing 1, 2022

PROLOGUE

Unless an asteroid hits the planet sometime in August, this summer will *not* be the end of the world.

Trust me, girls. You're going to be fine. Mom promise.

Tina, I know you're going to sleepaway camp FOR THE FIRST TIME EVER! (Sorry about the shouting. I know I should probably use my indoor voice.)

But you'll have fun.

You'll swim, go on hikes, paddle canoes, shoot arrows (at the targets only, please), and meet all sorts of new friends. I never got to go to a regular summer camp when I was your age. It's why I still don't know the recipe for s'mores. I know graham crackers are involved. I sure wish I knew how to do something fun with graham crackers besides making gingerbread houses that nobody ever wants to eat because the graham cracker walls taste like plasterboard.

And Grace, I understand your anxiety because you're going to SOCCER CAMP. But you're very good at soccer. A superstar!

Me?

I still don't understand why you have to use your feet all the time and can't just scoop up the ball with your hands and toss it into the gooooooooal!!! You can use your hands in football and, hello, it's called *foot*ball.

But you, Grace, are amazingly talented. The best soccer player your dad and I have ever seen, and don't forget, we watched that soccer movie *She's the Man* twice. And, yes, all the other kids at Camp Super Soccer Stars will also be extremely good at kicking, chipping, covering, and crossing. But remember— they put their knee socks on one leg at a time, just like you. And I think they put their shin guards on before they do that. Not sure. Need to do a little more research on that one.

But first, to ease your fears, I want to tell you guys

one more story from *my* exciting summer of 1991.

This took place in August, to be precise. After my big Shakespearean debut. After a few of my sisters had fallen in love. After I'd helped Dad land his first job with the Seaside Heights Police Department. After I'd climbed the Ferris wheel a couple of times to howl at the moon.

I was facing something like what you guys are facing. I was certain my world, as I knew it, was about to come to an end.

But I survived. I'm still here. I've been on *Saturday Night Live*, I've starred in a few TV shows, I won an Academy Award, and Jamie Grimm, the funniest kid on the planet, is my close, personal friend.

Still, believe it or not, my career almost ended before it even got started.

CHAPTER 1

Okay, girls, like I said, it's still the summer of 1991. I'm twelve years old.

It's August. What they call "the dog days." It's so hot, cows are giving evaporated milk. It's so hot, New York City asked the Statue of Liberty to lower her arm. It's so hot, I'm panting like Sandfleas, our dog, and wishing I could shed my fur the way she does every summer. I also wouldn't mind splashing around in my little sister Emma's kiddie pool.

Fortunately, the Super Soaker squirt gun was everywhere in 1991. Very refreshing.

And, in August 1991, the minimum wage is $4.25 per hour.

I know this because that's how much my boss, Vinnie, is paying me at the Balloon Race booth on the boardwalk in Seaside Heights, New Jersey, where I have a summer job. It's a pretty goofy game. You aim a metal squirt gun at a clown's tiny mouth. When you nail the spinning target between his teeth, a balloon attached to the pointy tip of the clown's hat starts to inflate. First balloon to get blown up so big that it actually blows up wins.

Now, as you might recall, June and July were

filled with excitement, intrigue, and romance. I was in a professional production of *A Midsummer Night's Dream* starring the international superstar Latoya Sherron (I think she hangs out with Mariah Carey on a regular basis). I helped my dad bust a notorious graffiti tagger. And, fortunately, not much of that romantic junk happened to me in June or July. Cupid's arrow bull's-eyed my big sisters Hannah (she's fourteen), Victoria (she's fifteen), and Sophia (the second-oldest, she's eighteen).

In August, all of that is over. Well, not all the romances. Some of those are still going on. (I know, gross.)

But my *Dream* show family has scattered. There is nothing fun or exciting to look forward to. Just another long month of hot work, setting up balloons and squirt guns for all the tourists flocking to Seaside Heights for their summer vacations. After that? School! BLEH. (Well, except for the drama club. And my friends. And those corn dogs in the cafeteria...)

Did I mention that we're having a horrible heat wave?

At nine o'clock in the morning, it's already ninety-some degrees with ninety percent humidity. My T-shirt is permanently glued to my spine with sweat. There's no breeze—just swarms of vicious, skin-biting flies known as greenheads.

By noon, I'm afraid I might melt. My hair is so damp and stringy, it looks like I'm wearing a wet mop on my head. My spiel to attract customers has lost most of its zing and all of its sparkle.

"Win a Tweety for your sweetie," I drone wearily. "Take home a Bart for your sweetheart. Step right up and squirt a clown. Show Bozo there's a new sheriff in town."

Finally, I have eight sweaty shooters all lined up.

I have an audience! The show must go on and so must I!

I bop the button and ring the bell. Water gushes through hoses and up into the pistols. In a flash, there are eight jets of cool, refreshing liquid arcing from the nozzles of the squirt guns to the clown targets four feet away. I imagine I am in Rome! My Balloon Race booth becomes the Trevi Fountain from the Oscar-winning movie *Three Coins in the Fountain*!

I start singing, pretending I'm that Jersey Shore favorite, Frank Sinatra.

"Three coins in the fountain!" I warble.

The crowd gawks at me, their jaws hanging open. Clearly, they are mesmerized and demand more!

As I sing on, I skip and twirl and dance my way up and down the water fountain firing line, tossing pennies over my shoulder. I'm also getting totally soaked by the players, pausing to let some of the squirt gun water shoot directly into *my* mouth instead of a clown's. I'm having a blast getting blasted.

And then, like always, I go too far. I add a coin-flinging spin. A very balletic pirouette.

All that water that's splashing off me is also pooling and puddling on the floor.

I slip.

I fall.

I land on my butt.

Now half the boardwalk is laughing. Not with me. *At* me.

Yep. It's just like when I was back in pre-K and stuttered every time I tried to say my name. Jacky Hart came out as Jacky Ha-Ha-Ha-Hart, which is how, thanks to some five-year-old bullies named Bubblebutt and Ringworm, I quickly became known as Jacky Ha-Ha. That nickname stuck with me like bubblegum on the sole of my shoe.

And the shooter at the counter laughing the loudest when I slip and fall?

It's Bubblebutt.

CHAPTER 2

Okay, Bubblebutt's real name is Bob Brownkowski, and believe it or not, in the summer of 1991, he's trying his hardest to reform his ways and become a decent human being.

He's still a big, beefy kid who buys his clothes off what JCPenney calls the "husky" rack, but he's no longer the bully he was back in kindergarten, when he hung me upside down on the jungle gym with my nose hovering six inches above a fire-ant mound. Bob actually helped me out that summer. His old friend and partner-in-bullying Ringworm? Not so much.

Anyway, I can't blame Bob for laughing at me

like that. Even though I look completely ridiculous, I don't want to stand back up. This shaded puddle of water on the balloon booth floor is very refreshing. Like a waterbed filled with ice cubes.

But I have to get back to work. Vinnie isn't paying me that whopping four and a quarter bucks an hour to sit on my butt. That's *his* job. He has a squeaky stool with a foam rubber seat patched with duct tape that he perches on all summer long.

Bob leans over the counter to give me a hand and hoists me up to my feet.

"Thanks, Bob," I say.

"No problemo, Jacky," he says.

I sniff my hand. It smells like Calvin Klein cologne. I think Bob collects those scented sample cards that fall out of magazines and rubs them on his face whenever he casually drops by my booth to pop a few balloons.

"Hey, Bob?" I say. "What're you doing later on?"

He shrugs. "I dunno." I think he's playing it cool. Maybe he read about doing that in one of those scented magazines.

All day long, while I've been doing my spiel and

setting up the balloon races, I've been staring at the T-Shirt Hut on the other side of the boardwalk. The usual suspects are there. The STUPID and I'M WITH STUPID shirts with their pointing fingers. The shirts that say FBI: FULL-BLOODED ITALIAN. Cartoon character shirts.

But one really catches my eye. It has a funny quote emblazoned on its chest:

BE YOURSELF; EVERYONE ELSE IS ALREADY TAKEN.

Yes, that's where I have my major aha moments in life: the T-shirt racks of a souvenir shop.

That shirt really speaks to me. Everything snaps into focus.

Who am I trying to kid? I'm never going to be a Shakespearean actor with a phony British accent. That isn't the real me. The whole *Midsummer Night's Dream* thing was a fluke. And, yes, I've been in a show with Latoya Sherron, but I'm never going to be the next Latoya Sherron.

I need to be me.

Jacqueline Hart. Daughter of Mac and Sydney Hart. A kid from a Jersey Shore town who'll never be much more than a kid from a Jersey Shore town, and unlike that other Jersey Shore kid known as the Boss, Bruce Springsteen, I don't think I'm born to run. I was born to stay. I'm a boardwalk barker. A practical joker. A class clown cutup.

Once, at a 7-Eleven, I pumped mustard and pickle relish into the bottom of a Slurpee cup, sprinkled that gunk with salt and pepper, swirled in a frosty red slush pile from the Slurpee dispenser, stuck in a straw, and gave it to my friend Bill Phillips. When he sucked in a little taste of that custom-crafted smooth refresher, he started gacking. I claimed it was a new flavor: Cherry Mustard Pickle Pepper.

I thought I was hysterical. Bill didn't. Neither did my best friend, Meredith.

But I was just being me. The only me I know how to be.

It's like I have a little angel and devil sitting on opposite shoulders. The devil is constantly poking and prodding me to do wild stuff—like that Slurpee stunt. Meanwhile, the angel on my other shoulder seems to enjoy taking time off. Sometimes, she's just not there to steer me in the right direction. I think she watches a lot of TV.

Anyway, it's so unrelentingly hot and humid and stifling and boring, I know I need to do something to shake things up. I need to break out of the dog day doldrums.

So I tell Bob to meet me when I get off work that afternoon. He does.

"Let's do something ka-ray-zee," I tell him as I step out of the booth at five.

"Okay," says Bob. He's up for anything. "How

about we dare each other to eat one of everything on the boardwalk?"

I shake my head. "Been there. Done that."

Just then, the devil perched on my shoulder has a really good, horrible idea.

"But...how about we eat something greasy and ride a ride. Then we eat something worse and ride another ride?"

Bob's goofy grin widens—all the way across his face. "I like it. We keep going until one of us pukes. Instead of a Battle of the Bands, we'll have a Battle of the Barfs."

I shake his hand. "Whoever blows chunks first loses!"

"Deal!"

"Game on!"

I can't wait. This is going to be the best boardwalk day ever!

CHAPTER 3

Bob and I have a blast eating our way up and down the boardwalk.

Come on, who doesn't love an Italian sausage sandwich? It's a soggy hoagie bun stuffed with spiced pork, greasy grilled peppers (green and red for the Italian flag), and glassy (also greasy) onion slices.

"Give me mine with sweet sausage," I tell the guy scooting and scraping all the ingredients around with a spatula on a sputtering grill.

"Nuh-uh," says Bob. "Hot and spicy. Two of 'em."

Oooh. He's upping the stakes. The guy is serious about this barf-a-thon.

"Challenge accepted," I say.

We wolf down our sandwiches and, feeling

bloated, hurry to the Mad Mouse roller coaster.

It's a tight track with wicked sharp turns. Every time you fly into a curve, you think you're going to rocket off the edge and die. Just when you recover, the little mouse car whips into another turn, throws you another curve, and you think you're about to die all over again.

It's a blast.

It also returns those Italian sausage sandwiches to the backs of our throats. We get to taste it all over again, but neither one of us hurls, heaves, or tosses our cookies.

We move on to a pizza stand.

Bob ups the stakes, again. "No slices, Jacky. We each have to eat a whole calzone!"

Calzones are like folded-over pizza dough pop-overs stuffed with ricotta and mozzarella cheese plus salami and ham. Talk about a belly bomb.

We each choke one down.

Next ride—the swinging pirate ship.

It's an open gondola, designed to look like, you guessed it, a pirate ship. It swings back and forth. Back and forth. Higher and higher. It's kind of like being on a seesaw and a swing at the same time.

The ride glides to its end and we stumble out of our seats.

But I do not spew the spumoni. Neither does Bob. So it's time for dessert.

We go to a bakery that sells giant cookies the size of manhole covers. These jumbo chocolate chip cookies are topped with sprinkles and chunks of other cookies: Oreos, Nutter Butters, Animal Crackers, Chips Ahoy.

We break the cookie in two and share it.

Bob looks a little green around the gills as we waddle up the boardwalk to the next ride. I catch my reflection in a mirror at the top of a rotating sunglasses display. I look even greener. We're talking Kermit the Frog green.

All of a sudden, our "best boardwalk day ever" doesn't feel so besty anymore.

CHAPTER 4

You wanna call it a tie?" groans Bob as we make our way to our next ride: the dreaded Gravitron.

I shake my head. "Nope. A tie is like kissing your sister."

"Which one?" says Bob, wiggling his eyebrows. "You've got a bunch of 'em!"

That earns Bob a knuckle punch in the arm.

"I deserved that," he says.

He's right. He did.

If any ride is going to make one of us lose our lunch (or early supper), it'll be the Gravitron.

It's decorated to look like a spaceship, but it's basically a big whirling barrel.

It reminds me of the spin cycle in a washing machine.

The barrel reaches a rotation rate of twenty-four rpm in a flash—less than twenty seconds. All that rotating creates centrifugal force—an outward pull that glues you to the padded walls like a limp pair of soggy socks. Once you're pinned in place, the floor drops out from beneath your feet.

Bob and I take side-by-side positions.

"Good luck, Jacky," he says. Then he belches. His breath smells like salami, pepperoni, garlic, peanut butter, and Animal Crackers. It's pretty gross. Until I burp and smell my own breath. It's worse. There are definitely Tic Tacs in my future. Maybe a whole rattling box of 'em.

The ride starts up.

In no time, we're both glued to the wall. My stomach is being pulled back toward my spine. My cheeks are flapping. I feel like I'm undergoing NASA astronaut training, which, by the way, is probably like swimming. You shouldn't do it for an hour after eating.

My legs feel like rubber noodles when, finally, the barrel spins to a stop and the exit doors slide open.

We stumble out to the boardwalk.

Bob doesn't barf.

But I do.

I lurch forward and retch up everything. I literally blow chunks. Chocolate chip chunks. Sausage hunks. Calzone lumps. A colorful reminder of all the delicious food I've snarfed down in less than an hour.

And I'm not looking where I'm spewing.

I'm just bent over, wishing there was a toilet in the middle of the boardwalk instead of some dude.

All I see are his knobby knees, his socks, and his Nikes.

And the mess I'm making all over the tips of his kicks.

Finally, when I feel like I've heaved my last load, I look up.

It's Bill Phillips.

He of the crazy-gorgeous hazel eyes. The boy that I have a kind-of, sort-of crush on. Hey, I'm twelve going on thirteen. It's summer. It happens. Even to me.

"Uh, hi, Bill." Bob says it first. "Just so you know, bro—Jacky and I aren't on a date or anything."

The way he says it, it sounds like *I mean, why would anybody in their right mind want to go on a date with Jacky Ha-Ha?*

My mouth is too gross for me to speak. So I give Bill a finger-wiggle wave and a sad puppy dog look to say sorry. And not just for what I did to his shoes. (His Air Jordans look like Scare Jordans.)

"Well, Jacky, I gotta book," says Bob. "Let's do this again. Not!"

He runs away as fast as he can.

Bill slides the sides of his sneaks along the boardwalk planks. That scrapes off the big stuff. Then he dumps his jumbo-sized soda and ice on the mess to wash it away.

"Wish I'd brought along one of the squirt guns from the Balloon Race booth," I try to joke, which is much harder to do when you're feeling queasy and smelling cheesy.

Bill steps back a pace or two. I think he just got a whiff of my Jif, to borrow a line from a peanut butter commercial.

Bill shakes his head. I think he's disappointed in me. Not as disappointed as I am in myself, but close.

"Haven't you played this scene before?" he asks.

"Yeah. A couple times."

"Jacky?"

"Yeah, Bill?"

"I think you might need a new script."

Yes, girls. Your father was always the wisest, smartest—not to mention sweetest—boy in the whole state of New Jersey, even when we were twelve.

CHAPTER 5

Things are hot and boring for me and my sisters at home, too.

There are six of us Hart girls currently residing in Seaside Heights. Think of us as Little Women down the Jersey Shore. Only none of us owns an ankle-length dress or a shoulder cape.

Which is a good thing. Dad didn't put the AC units in the windows of our tiny beach bungalow this summer. Our house is an oven. My parents are saving money because, even though Dad already has an offer to become a full-time cop right after Labor Day, in August he's still working as a very low-paid "auxiliary cop." The SHPD doesn't even issue him a real police hat. Just a navy blue baseball cap.

Meanwhile, Mom, back from her service in Iraq (the First Gulf War, the one they called Desert Storm), is going to cop school at a nearby community college. She is earning zero dollars a week but spending a bunch of money on books and other college stuff.

That's why any Hart girl who is old enough to have a work permit also has a summer job on the boardwalk.

In addition to our day jobs, my sisters and I are in charge of housecleaning and meal prep. Even on days when, according to the radio, it's "steamy, sweltering, and sweaty."

"It's so muggy out, you can wear the air while it frizzes your hair!" says Hannah, cooling herself off in front of the open refrigerator. Hannah is fourteen and super-sweet. She's working her dream job at the Fudgery. Well, it was a dream until they started docking her paycheck for the free samples she kept nibbling. "How else am I supposed to know what all the different flavors taste like?" she asked her bosses.

They told her to use her imagination.

"Quit your bellyaching, Hannah," barks Emma.

"Oorah! We need to whip this house into tip-top condition fifteen minutes prior to fifteen minutes prior!" Emma is six. We call her the Little Boss. Our mom was a marine. We think Emma might've inherited every single one of Mom's marine genes.

Victoria (don't you dare call her Vickie) is fifteen going on fifty. She thinks the rest of us are "sooooo immature." She has a job at Willy B. Williams's Taffy Shoppe. She also has an opinion about everything because, well, she already knows everything there is to know. Someday, I think they might name the local library after her. She's their biggest reader.

"Everybody?" Victoria says between flicks of her feather duster. "Just a quick reminder: Be sure to circle May twenty-third on your calendars."

"Why?" I ask, because somebody has to. "This is August. It won't be May again until next year."

"But, you guys? May twenty-third is National Taffy Day!"

"Seriously?" says Sophia. "How does everybody celebrate? By combing sticky clumps of goo out of their hair?"

Sophia is eighteen and the second-oldest or, as she likes to put it, the "oldest sister still living at home," because Sydney, who's nineteen, is in college at Princeton, which is also in New Jersey, by the way. Sophia has found her "one true love" at least a dozen times. Just this summer.

Then there's Riley. She's eleven. One year younger than me. That's why I kind of feel sorry for her. Technically, she should look up to me. See me as a role model. But, as Bob or Bill or that devil on my shoulder will gladly tell you, I can be a very bad influence. I know *I* sure wouldn't want to be my little sister.

Anyway, after a hard day of work, we're all putting in another few hard hours of housework. Under the stern and unblinking eye of Emma, we're scrubbing toilets, dusting every dustable surface, vacuuming sand out of the rugs, and mopping more sand off the floors. Sandfleas, our beloved mutt, is right there with us. She likes to chase the mop and snarl at the vacuum.

But everybody's exhausted. And sweaty. Yes, all our shorts are currently sweatshorts; our shirts, sweatshirts. Our un-air-conditioned house is a sauna.

"I can't take this anymore," moans Hannah.

"Yes you can, worm!" barks Emma. She's definitely

drill sergeant material. "Work isn't supposed to be fun. That's why they call it work!"

Emma gives me an idea.

Maybe work *can* be fun! We could turn our chores into a song-and-dance routine, like something out of a Broadway musical! We can choreograph our cleaning moves to a cool tune. So I dig through Mom and Dad's collection of records (those are round vinyl things that make music when you scratch a needle through their grooves—look it up).

I find the perfect tune: "Car Wash" by Rose Royce. It's the Golden Globe–nominated original song from the 1976 movie *Car Wash* starring Richard Pryor and George Carlin. (I'm guessing Mom and Dad saw it on a date or something, back when Dad was Mac Hart, "the best-looking boy on the beach," and thanks to Mom, he had the T-shirt to prove it.)

I spin the disc and crank up the volume.

"Come on, Hart girls!" I shout. "I need everybody to get up, get up, get up! I need some en-er-gy! Come on, now!"

Before long, we're all movin' and shakin', dancing our way through the drudgery.

The whole house is white-glove clean in less than an hour. We're ready for inspection.

But Dad has to work a double shift. And Mom has to hit the college library.

We're on our own for dinner.

"How about pizza?" I suggest with a wink to Emma. "Cheese pizza."

Cheese pizza is the only kind my six-year-old sister will eat. And usually, it's her first food choice. Breakfast, lunch, or dinner.

"No," she says, stomping her feet on the squeaky-clean floor. "It's too darn hot."

Wow. Emma saying no to pizza? I guess there's a first time for everything.

"O-kay," I say. "How about cereal? It's nice and cold."

"Yes!" everybody agrees.

So we have a Froot Loops and Fruity Pebbles feast!

And while we're all gathered around the table eating, a true miracle takes place.

There is actually a hint of a breeze blowing through the screens in the windows and our open back door.

CHAPTER 6

ater that week, I'm walking back to work on the boardwalk.

The heat is unrelenting. It's so hot, I wouldn't be surprised if all the sand on the beach has turned into glass. The air is heavy, too. It weighs down all the smells from all the food stalls. The aromas are trapped in some kind of invisible, nose-level cloud. And, after my barf-a-thon with Bob, there's no worse odor in the world than sizzling Italian sausage sandwiches. Except for maybe garlicky ham-and-salami calzones. Or chocolate chip cookies the size of a spare tire.

My stomach is doing flips and flops. I will never do anything that ridiculous again. I'm actually making a pinkie swear with myself when, all of a sudden, somebody, a total stranger, recognizes me.

"Hey!" she says. "You're that girl. You put on quite a show!"

I perk up. Smile modestly. "I take it you saw me playing Puck at Shakespeare Down the Shore in June?"

"Huh? Shakespeare?"

"Yes," I say, with just the hint of a British accent. "I was Puck in *A Midsummer Night's Dream*."

"Nah, I didn't see it," says the girl I've never met before with a snap and pop of her chewing gum. "But you were definitely the girl puking up chunks of gunk all over that poor dude's new Nikes on the boardwalk the other day. Now that was some show! Hilarious. Are you going to be doing a repeat performance anytime soon? Because my friends that I'm staying with, they missed the first show and—"

I walk away. Fast.

I make a beeline for the Balloon Race booth.

Where two mysterious women in sunglasses and headscarves are waiting for me.

One I recognize immediately as Ms. O'Mara, my English teacher, drama club director, and all-around mentor. Ms. O'Mara knows tons about theater. She starred in *Annie* on Broadway when she was a kid. She was also in my *Midsummer Night's Dream* cast. Oh, who am I kidding. It was really her *Dream* cast. She helped put the whole Shakespeare Down the Shore thing together.

And standing with her—with not only a headscarf but a baseball cap pulled down tight to her humongous sunglasses—is, I'm pretty sure, Ms. O'Mara's longtime friend and former *Annie* castmate, Latoya Sherron.

That's right. *The* Latoya Sherron. The same Latoya Sherron who's won three Grammys, a couple of Tony Awards, and an Oscar for Best Original Song (it wasn't the one from *Car Wash*). She's wearing the hat, the scarf, and the sunglasses so she can try to stay incognito. To blend in with the crowd and go unrecognized.

Which is super-hard for her to do.

A lot of the shops and stalls on the boardwalk have all sorts of Latoya Sherron merchandise. T-shirts (some have sequins and glitter; others are airbrushed like a black velvet painting), posters, and bobblehead dolls. Her summer song "You Can't Beat the Heat of My Heartbeat" is number one on all the charts and is constantly blasting out of speakers and nightclubs all over Seaside Heights.

Think about the biggest pop star you know. In 1991, Latoya Sherron is twice as popular. She's bigger than Paula Abdul, Mariah Carey, Olivia Newton-John, and Vanilla Ice combined. Okay, everybody's bigger than Vanilla Ice, but you get the picture. Ms. O'Mara and Ms. Sherron don't see me yet. They're just chitchatting.

"So how's your daughter?" I hear Ms. O'Mara ask Ms. Sherron.

"She's doing great. What's the four-one-one on that guy you were seeing in the city?"

Ms. O'Mara shakes her head and laughs. "Don't go there."

"You should bring him to see my new show. We start previews in a couple weeks."

"You're at the Alvin Theater?"

"Yep. Our old stomping grounds…"

I'm, of course, wondering what a mega-superstar triple-threat singer-dancer-actor like Latoya Sherron is doing back in town. Sure, she was in Seaside Heights for the Shakespeare show, but like I said, that was weeks ago.

"Ms. O'Mara?" I say. "Ms. Sherron? Latoya Sherron?"

Oops.

The minute I say her name, heads whip around. A lot of those heads are poking up out of those Latoya Sherron T-shirts I told you about.

The boardwalk erupts in shrieks.

"Squeeee!"

"It's her!"

"That's Latoya Sherron!"

"I need to get my bobblehead doll autographed!"

"Will you sign my shirt?"

Ms. Sherron is mobbed. The Sharpies come out. She's signing everything anybody shoves at her. (I'm not sure why one guy wants a Latoya Sherron–autographed baseball, but he does.)

"Sorry," I say. "My bad. Come on. I know a place where we can hide!"

CHAPTER 7

The Beachcomber is the sit-down restaurant where my sister Sophia has her summer job.

It's why she comes home smelling like a hamburger with a side of onion rings all the time. The Beachcomber is open only for lunch and dinner, but Sophia is already on the job in the morning, refilling ketchup bottles and saltshakers.

Sophia sees me and the two ladies in sunglasses and headscarves dashing toward the restaurant. She hurries into the lobby, twists the lock, and opens the door. Ms. Sherron and Ms. O'Mara tumble in. I stand at the door and address the crowd while Sophia plays hostess and finds her unexpected guests a booth in the back, far away from the front windows.

"We're so glad you guys could chase us across the boardwalk," I tell the mob outside the restaurant. They're all eagerly waving things they want Ms. Sherron to sign. "Ms. Sherron is flattered that you chose to mob her instead of the Boss."

"Bruce Springsteen?" someone shouts.

"Is he here, too?" screams someone else.

"Not sure," I say. "But, rumor has it, Bruce loves to play Skee-Ball. With Jon Bon Jovi."

I glance over at the nearby arcade. The crowd sees me glancing.

They put two and two together, jump to conclusions, and take off—hot on the trail of the Jersey Shore's biggest rock stars. Yep, they're born to run in a blaze of glory.

When I'm sure the Latoya Sherron fans have dispersed, I make my way to the back of the restaurant. Sophia's boss is posing for a photo with Ms. Sherron. Sophia snaps it for him on his fancy digital camera. (In 1991, if anybody said a phone could take pictures, they would've been laughed out of the room.)

"Can I get youse young ladies anything?" Sophia's smiling boss asks Ms. Sherron and Ms. O'Mara.

"No thank you, Sam," says Ms. Sherron.

The owner of the Beachcomber blushes. "You remembered my name."

"Of course I did, Sam. You're very unforgettable."

Now Sam is beaming. "You ladies stay here as long as you like. Sophia? They need anything, you give it to 'em. On the house."

"Yes, sir, Mr. Doshi," says Sophia. She shoots me a wink and goes back to tipping ketchup bottles into ketchup squeezers. I think we just earned her some brownie points with her boss.

Ms. O'Mara motions for me to join her and Ms. Sherron in the booth. Phew. They aren't mad at me for blowing their cover.

I slide into the vinyl bench opposite them.

"You did good out there with the crowd," says Ms. Sherron.

"Thanks. I just sort of improvised."

Ms. O'Mara nods. She's the one who taught me how to create a scene out of nothing.

"You're very talented, Jacky," Ms. Sherron continues. "And now it's time to up your game."

"Well," I said, "I really don't play many of the games on the boardwalk. They won't let me because I know how to beat them. Like the Ringtoss. All you really have to do is bend down low and..."

I stop because both women are shaking their heads.

"That's not what Latoya's talking about," says Ms. O'Mara. "We came to the boardwalk today to find you. We think you should go to camp."

"Seriously?" I say. "Like hiking and swimming and arts and crafts?"

"Just that last bit," says Ms. Sherron. "Your art and your craft. You have raw talent. But talent is nothing without hard work and training. I think you should do like I did when I was your age."

"You want me to win a Grammy Award?" I say.

Ms. Sherron smiles. "No. That came a few years later. When I was your age, I went to Camp Footlights. It's a performing arts training center outside New York City. A wonderful place to push yourself beyond your comfort zone. To learn valuable skills."

"It's also in a beautiful woodsy setting," adds Ms. O'Mara. She shows me a brochure. There are all sorts of pictures of kids my age or a little older. They're singing. They're dancing. They're putting on shows. They look like they're having fun.

And they all look ten times more talented than I'll ever be!

CHAPTER 8

I quickly discover, over free iced tea courtesy of Sophia and her boss, Mr. Doshi, that Ms. Sherron will not take no for an answer.

"You need to do this, Jacky."

"B-b-but…" Yes. I'm stammering again. If this pressure keeps up, I may stumble all the way back to my old stutter.

"There's a new three-week session starting this weekend," Ms. Sherron tells me. "I still have a few friends on the board of directors."

"She's being modest," says Ms. O'Mara, smiling toward Ms. Sherron. "Latoya is the camp's most famous alum."

"I wouldn't say that. Don't forget—Caroline Jean Risvold went to Camp Footlights, too."

My eyes go wide. "Caroline Jean Risvold?" I kind of gasp it. "The one they call Copper because of her blazing red hair? The star of all those movies? She was in that one with Kevin Costner and that other one with Bruce Willis!"

Ms. Sherron nods. "Caroline Jean Risvold was a Camp Footlighter. Of course, I just called her Copper. We did a couple shows together. And, Jacky? You don't have to worry about any of the camp costs. I'm going to pay for the whole thing."

Now my jaw drops. "Y-y-you are?"

Ms. Sherron smiles at me. "Yep. It's payback time. Back in the day, an anonymous angel paid for me to become a Camp Footlighter. I still don't know who it was...."

I start wondering if I can ask the little angel on my shoulder to do some digging. Find out which one of her friends did Ms. Sherron such a solid when she was a kid. Then I realize that imaginary shoulder angels probably don't know any real angels, except the kind they've seen as Hummel figurines in the boardwalk souvenir shops.

"So what do you say?" asks Ms. O'Mara. She's beaming at me.

"I, well, I d-d-don't kn-kn-know wh-wh-what t-t-to s-s-say...."

Oh, yeah. My stutter is back and making up for lost time.

"Breathe," says Ms. O'Mara. "I know it's a lot to take in."

"It's a v-v-very ge-ge-generous offer."

Now Ms. Sherron motions for me to sip my tea. I do. It gives me the time I need to remember some of the stutter-busting strategies Ms. O'Mara taught me.

Speak slowly. Speaking slowly and deliberately can reduce stress and the symptoms of a stutter.

So I slow everything down. I think there are turtles and sloths who speak faster.

"I...really...appreciate...the...offer," I say. Several ice cubes melt in my tea during the time it takes me to say those five words without hitting any speed bumps. "But..."

Ms. Sherron smiles. "But what?"

"Well…"

I'm doing okay on the wicked *W*, so I pick up my pace just a little.

"I promised my mom and dad that I'd earn money for our f-f-family this summer."

Ms. O'Mara turns to Ms. Sherron. "Her parents are training for their new careers. Not earning a ton of money."

I feel another splutter coming on, so I slow back down. "That…is…correct."

"Not to worry," says Ms. Sherron. "I'll make up for the three weeks of income you'll lose while you're at camp."

"Th-th-three w-w-weeks?"

Yep. That one completely stresses me out again.

"That's how long your camp session will last," she explains. "And think about it—if you're not at home, your family's food bill will go down."

Maybe, I think. *But not if Sophia just picks up my mealtime slack.*

I'm a stress stutterer. She's a stress eater. Victoria, on the other hand, is just a stress transmitter.

"Plus," I say, "I think I may be allergic to lanyards."

Both women raise skeptical eyebrows.

"You, uh, have to make lanyards at camp, right?"

Now they both laugh and shake their heads.

"No," says Ms. O'Mara. "This is a *showbiz* camp. No lanyards required. No s'mores, either."

"Just a lot of rehearsing and performing," adds Ms. Sherron. "There's a new show every week."

"Riiiight. But, well, uh, you see I was, uh, really hoping to work on my sand collection this summer...."

Yes, I collect bottles of sand from all over. Mom even brought me some from Saudi Arabia.

The sand-collection remark earns me an eye roll from Ms. O'Mara and a disappointed sigh from Ms. Sherron. They can see right through me. They know I'm clutching at straws, and not just the one bobbing up and down in my iced tea. I'm making up reasons I can't go to Camp Footlights because, basically, I'M PETRIFIED!

All those uber-talented kids? No way am I at their level. I mean, seriously, did you see that brochure? Those triple-threat talents are all miniature Latoya Sherrons. Me? I'm just Jacky Ha-Ha.

"Look," says Ms. Sherron, sounding disappointed and, frankly, a little frustrated. "At Camp Footlights, you'll be seeing Broadway shows. Performing in a new showcase every week. Writing your own material. You'll also be around kids who will challenge and push you. The staff and teachers are all terrific. The camp director, Mr. Beasley, is somewhat new, but I'm sure he's a superstar, too. Jacky, this is a seriously major opportunity. It may not knock on your door again."

She's right. I know it. So I nod.

"Can I think about it?" I say. "Talk it over with my family?"

"Of course," says Ms. Sherron. "But I need your answer tomorrow. Mr. Beasley is holding a slot for you, but he has a waiting list a mile long."

Oh, good, I think.

If I say no, some other kid will get a chance to say yes.

So, by not going to Camp Footlights, I'd actually be doing a good deed for a stranger.

Right?

Somehow, I don't think anybody would buy that

excuse. Not even the imaginary angel sitting on my shoulder.

CHAPTER 9

That afternoon, at home, my sisters help me come up with more reasons I can't take Ms. Sherron's generous offer.

"Have you ever read the statistics about camp-related illnesses and injuries?" says Victoria. "I have. You can break a leg falling off a horse or playing capture the flag. You can also get a headache, nausea, a fever, or…"

She looks around before she whispers the next word.

"Diarrhea! That's because too many campers swallow lake water or eat camp food, which, by the way, might also explain some of that nausea I mentioned."

"You *could* pack fudge to eat instead of camp food, but it'd melt in your suitcase," says Hannah. "Trust me. I know. I tried it that time we took the overnight trip to see our cousins in Philly...."

"You can't go to Camp Footfights," says Riley. "That sounds horrible. Do other campers stomp on your feet all the time?"

"It's Camp Footlights," I tell her. "Foot*lights*, not footfights."

"Oh. Never mind."

I tell Riley that footlights are those lights you sometimes see aiming up at performers from the front lip of a stage. "Camp Footlights is like a training camp for showbiz kids."

Riley's eyes go wide as she finally figures out what I'm saying. "But you still can't go, Jacky. We need you to stay here. If you go to sleepaway camp, who'd choreograph our nightly housecleaning dance routine?"

Victoria raises her hand. "I could do that. I'd just need to read a few books on the subject. Watch a few more Paula Abdul videos. Besides, I'm not sure 'Car Wash' is the best choice of dramatic dance music...."

"I think you *should* go, Jacky," says Sophia. "Hey,

I know if Latoya Sherron asked me to do *anything*, I'd do it! Plus, there might be some *boys* at this camp." She wiggle-waggles her eyebrows. To make things worse, she picks up a couch pillow, squeezes it tight, and gives it a big smooch right on its button.

So my family isn't much help in the decision-making department.

After dinner (more cold cereal plus even colder ice cream for dessert—Mom and Dad both had to work late again), I think about my gang of theater buddies.

Who says we can't run our own showbiz camp—right on the boardwalk?

The boards will be our stage! The milling summer crowds of tourists and day-trippers will be our audience! Bill's cassette player will be our orchestra! This way, I can work on my art and my craft without talking to Mom and Dad about camp, leaving my job, or trying to impress a bunch of super-talented theater kids.

So, to get my idea rolling right away, I call up my pals from the drama club shows and *A Midsummer Night's Dream*: Dan Napolitano, Jeff Cohen, Bill Phillips, Schuyler Cooke, and Meredith Crawford. We'll do our first show that night!

Meredith, my BFF since forever, is an amazing singer. Which is why, it turns out, she can't come to my camp. She's too busy packing her bags because, the very next day, she's heading off to her own arts camp.

"It's called Interlochen. It's in Michigan. They have a terrific music program! Latoya Sherron is giving me a full-ride scholarship to attend a four-week intensive! I leave tomorrow. I'm packing now but was going to call you right after. Ms. Sherron paid for the plane tickets, too!"

Well, what do you know, says the little devil on my shoulder. *Sounds like Ms. Sherron is hedging her bets. If you won't go to a fancy-pants performing arts camp this summer, at least Meredith will!*

Schuyler, who's a few years older than me and my other friends, will be a no-show, too. He and Sophia are going out tonight. Yeah—1991 was the year they became a thing. I guess that bit with the couch cushion was Sophia's dress rehearsal for her date.

Jeff Cohen is busy, too. "Duty calls," he tells me. "I have to wear my Bossy D. Cow costume tonight and hand out flyers. Heat waves are a gold rush for the ice cream biz, Jacky. It's udder madness!" Back in June, Jeff landed a job as the mascot for Swirl Tip Cones. It's why he's been saying stuff like "Have I ever *steered* you wrong?" all summer long.

That leaves Dan and Bill.

Except Dan isn't home.

"He went on vacation with his family," Bill tells me when I call him.

Bill, he of the gorgeous hazel eyes, is free. And he'll join me on the boardwalk for "whatever." I tell him to bring his cassette player.

"And some music!"

He does.

We set up shop right in front of the Ferris wheel.

"Let's start off with a big musical number!" I tell him.

"Um, okay. I have the original cast recording of *Cats*."

"Perfect!" I say. "Pop it in. This is going to be fun!"

I have no idea how wrong I am.

CHAPTER 10

The music starts up.

We pantomime a bunch of very gymnastic cat leaps, back arches, air-clawing scratches, and wide-open mouth hisses while the overture plays.

People strolling along the boardwalk do their best not to make eye contact with us. Most pick up their pace as they pass. Maybe they think Bill and I are members of some kind of crazed cat cult.

"Skip to track six!" I tell him when the overture mercifully ends.

A few ice cream cone lickers (guess Jeff's been doing a good job passing out his flyers) stop and gawk at us when we do the song "The Rum Tum Tugger." It's kind of like a rap, and we're having trouble keeping our lips flapping in sync with the fast-flying rat-a-tat lyrics.

Our mistakes are like human bloopers, which I think are pretty funny. The ice cream lickers don't agree. They don't pause to laugh. They just keep on licking.

"Kill the music," I tell Bill.

He hits the stop button on the cassette deck.

"Now what?" he asks.

"We tell some jokes!"

"I don't know any!"

"Just follow my lead."

"Okay," says Bill, because he's always been far too trusting, especially when it comes to me.

"Hey, Bill," I say, very loudly.

"Uh, yes, Jacky?"

"Why does a seagull fly over the sea?"

"I dunno, Jacky. Why does a seagull fly over the sea?"

"Because if it flew over the bay, it'd be a bay-gull." I tap out a *ba-boom-bop* rim shot on my thighs.

The guy selling Ferris wheel tickets is giving me a dirty look. I think we're scaring away his customers. Either that or he recognizes me as the notorious Ferris wheel climber.

We're definitely losing our crowd. Not that we ever actually had one.

But I refuse to give up. This is my performing arts training camp. In football, you need to take a few hard knocks at camp to improve your game. Same with show business.

"Hey, Bill?"

"Yeah?"

"What do you call a snowman in the summer?"

"A puddle," says a voice I don't recognize.

Because it's the guy from the Ferris wheel ticket booth. He's wearing a tank top, so the tops of his hairy shoulders are totally exposed. I don't think he's shaved in a few days, either. His face or his shoulders.

"You two are killing my business," he says, leaning in close so I can't not hear what he has to say. I also get a good whiff of *his* Jif. The guy's definitely a garlic knots fan.

"We're just—"

"Creating a public nuisance," the man tells us. "That's why we called the cops."

Two police officers come strolling up the boardwalk.

Well, technically, one of them isn't actually an officer. I can tell by his baseball cap that he's really just a summer auxiliary cop.

Yeah. It's my dad.

Dad's double shift? That night, some of it is spent giving Bill and me a stern warning.

"Don't do this again, you two."

We promise we won't.

Otherwise, I think our next comedy routine might be for all the folks locked up with us in the Seaside Heights jail.

CHAPTER 11

So my own personal performing arts camp idea flopped like a flipped pancake that ended up on the floor.

I bit the bullet and talked to Mom and Dad about Camp Footlights. Once they read the brochure and heard it was Latoya Sherron's idea and she would *pay* me to go, they were all the way on board.

But, the next morning, as I head to work at the Balloon Race booth, I convince myself that I don't need any kind of camp. Show business is just not meant to be my career. And it doesn't have to be. I'm already in an apprentice program for the very lucrative field of carnival barking. Okay, I don't know how lucrative it is. Remember, I'm making $4.25 an hour. I'm pretty sure most tycoons earn more than that.

But the boardwalk life has its perks. It's outdoor work, so you get plenty of sunshine and fresh air. You also get plenty of BO because sometimes that sunshine is hot and the fresh air muggy. But still.

Plus, the boardwalk is only really in business for three or four months. I could take the rest of the year off and do stuff. And when I'm done doing stuff, I could do things. My time would be my own. I'd probably end up with the best sand collection in all the land.

And, as the angel on my shoulder reminds me, Vinnie needs me. Sure, he's good at counting coins and making change, but I give the booth its sizzle with my snappy, comical patter. Before I came along, Vinnie was having a tough time corralling shooters interested in spending their hard-earned money just to squirt clowns in the mouth to see a balloon pop. Without me, he'd be lost. No way can I shirk my responsibilities and head off to Camp Footlights and leave Vinnie to face certain financial ruin.

I have a career! A future!

But then I see the booth.

There've been some big changes overnight.

For instance, the sign with all the chaser lights no longer says BALLOON RACE. There's a new sign. Apparently, the booth is now called Smack 'Em! Whack 'Em! The letters spelling it out are angry and snarling.

And the clown heads have all been covered with rubbery, open-mouthed Halloween masks. There are a couple of Darth Vaders and a few Hannibal Lecters, the psycho sicko from that *Silence of the Lambs* movie with Jodie Foster, which of course was one of the biggest box office blockbusters of 1991. Then there are a bunch of hockey-masked Jason heads from those *Friday the 13th* horror movies. My jolly (if creepy) row of clowns has been replaced by a rogues gallery of pop culture villains.

"Hey, Jacky?" Vinnie sees me gawping at the, uh, alterations. "Get over here. I want you to meet Anthony. He's gonna be your new boss."

I scurry over to the booth. The squirt gun pistols have been replaced, too. They're long-barrel assault rifles now.

"You the one they call Jacky Har-Dee-Har-Har?" says Anthony, a gruff guy wearing mirrored sunglasses. I don't correct him. I'm too busy studying his pencil-thin mustache and the three strands of oily hair he has combed over his otherwise bald dome.

"Yes, sir."

"I've seen you work the booth. You have lots of snappy patter. Jokes."

I smile a little. Sounds like the guy's a fan. "Yes, sir. That's me."

He shakes his head. "No it ain't. Not no more. You ain't gonna do no snappy patter no more. All you're gonna do is push this button."

He pushes a blinking red square on what looks like an 8-track tape deck. Suddenly, a synthesized voice that sounds an awful lot like a demonic monster snarls out of the new loudspeakers that must've been installed overnight, too. The rumbling monster voice is buried in a jumble of horrifying explosion and scream sound effects.

"Smack 'em, whack 'em, shoot 'em in the face! Watch their balloon brains explode as you save the human race!"

I'm feeling sick to my stomach again. This time, boardwalk food has nothing to do with it.

Finally, my new boss, Anthony, pushes the button to turn off the automated noisemaker.

"You don't say a word, Jacky Har-Dee-Har-Har. You just play that loop. Every five minutes."

Sure, I think. *No problem. I can do that. Besides, I really wanted to lose my mind this summer.*

I turn to Vinnie and give him my Bambi doe-eyed look. "You really sold the booth?"

He nods. "Yeah. I'm moving to New Mexico. It's a dry heat. Anthony here? He knows his stuff. Runs that paintball blaster booth over near the Taffy Shoppe. The one where you can blast and splat old cars and mannequins and teddy bears with paint-balls. You could learn a lot from him."

I nod.

I also reach into my pocket and pull out a crumpled one-dollar bill.

"Um, can you change this into four quarters?" I ask. "I need to make a quick phone call."

"Sure, kid."

Vinnie snatches my dollar, smooths it out, and finger-slides four quarters across the counter to me.

"Don't take too long, Jacky Har-Dee-Har-Har," Anthony snarls as I dash across the boardwalk to a cluster of pay phones. "I ain't paying you until you're in the booth making me some moola."

Which, of course, means he's never going to be paying me. Ever.

I drop in a quarter and make my call.

"Ms. O'Mara? It's me. Jacky. I wanted to thank you and Ms. Sherron for the amazingly generous offer. So, uh, when exactly do I leave for Camp Footlights?"

CHAPTER 12

O n Saturday morning, my sisters help Dad and me pack the car for the big trip to camp.

I don't have all the stuff that was on the suggested packing list.

For instance, tap shoes. I don't own a pair. So I packed my Sunday go-to-church Mary Janes and a cardboard sleeve of metal thumbtacks. I figure I can DIY my way to tap class. Of course, I'm not much of a hoofer anyway. That's what showbiz people call dancers, not mules.

"You'll be great!" Riley gushes as she helps me heave my suitcase into the trunk of Dad's car.

"Actually," says Victoria, "I've been doing some research...."

Of course she has.

"The kids at Camp Footlights are super-talented," she continues. "Don't get your hopes up too high, Jacky. Statistically, you're more likely to fail."

"So try to meet some cute boys," says Sophia.

"You sure you don't want some fudge for the ride?" asks Hannah. "I have peanut butter swirl."

"No thanks," I tell her.

Victoria looks at me and shakes her head. "I guess it's good you get this out of your system this summer. The sooner you crash and burn..."

Emma steps up. Her hands are on her hips.

"Jacky is not going to crash or burn or fail. She's going to be the biggest star at the whole camp. She's gonna teach 'em all how to do that 'Car Wash' dance!"

Yeah. I've always loved my littlest sister.

"Break a leg, hon," says Mom, using the theater expression for "good luck."

"And that's an order, young lady!" she adds in her booming marine voice.

I snap to attention and salute her. "Ma'am, yes, ma'am!"

"You'll be great, Jacky," says Riley as Dad closes the trunk.

Victoria rolls her eyes. "You're gonna fail, Jacky."

"So?" says Sophia. "If she fails, she'll be great at it. And she'll have more time to meet cute guys. Maybe even a future soap opera star!"

"We'll all come see you in your first show next Saturday!" says Hannah. "Right, Dad?"

"Yep," says my father. "We have it on the calendar. We'll all be there. Come on, kiddo. It's time we hit the road."

And so it's just me and my dad in the car. For a three-hour ride north to the suburbs outside New York City.

I don't think my father and I have ever spent three hours alone together. One-on-one time is impossible when you have six sisters. You're never really alone in the Hart house. Except in the bathroom. Sometimes.

We're cruising up the Garden State Parkway.

The ride is kind of quiet.

Neither one of us really knows how to talk to the other. Remember, we don't have much practice in the daughter-daddy chat department.

Finally, Dad says, "Nervous?"

"A little," I admit.

He nods. "I remember when I was playing ball in South Carolina. Got the call to join the Yankees farm team up in Oneonta. They told me to report to spring training camp. I was so jittery, Jacky. No, I was scared. Petrified! I wondered if I could even hold a bat without it shaking in my hands."

"Really? But you were incredible. You could hit, you could field."

Dad chuckles a little. "So could all the other guys being invited to try out for the team. I was going from being a big fish in a small pond to becoming a tiny guppy in an ocean full of superstars. The best of the best from all over North and South America."

Now it's my turn to nod. "That's how I'm feeling about Camp Footlights. It's a whole 'nother level of talent. A whole new league."

"Well, just remember, Jacky: Those other guys at baseball camp? They all put their cleats on one shoe at a time. Same with all the kids you're gonna meet at this camp."

"Um, we don't really wear cleats onstage."

"Well, how about those leotard things?"

"Sure. We wear those. Sometimes."

"And you pull them on one leg at a time?"

"Yes, sir."

"Well, Jacky, guess what? So does everybody else."

I smile as goose bumps tingle up and down my arms.

My baseball-playing, Jersey Shore–cop dad never really understood theater or show business or even comedy.

But he always tried to understand *me*.

I'm glad we had that time together in that first car ride up to Camp Footlights.

He tells me all sorts of stories and does his best to buck me up. To boost my confidence. And it's working.

I'm feeling better about my decision.

Until, of course, we pull through the Camp Footlights gates.

CHAPTER 13

The instant I say goodbye to Dad after check-in, I know I have made a HUGE, colossal, supersized mistake.

Yep. I should just run back down the road and chase after Dad. Too bad he's in a car. It's way faster than my feet.

I see all sorts of other Camp Footlighters scurrying around the main lodge building. Sure, they're all aged from ten to, like, eighteen, but some walk like elegant swans, as if they've had decades of ballet training. Others have so much bubbly energy, they'd put my cheery sister Hannah to shame. One girl is doing vocal warm-ups that make her sound like she's already starring in ten shows a week on Broadway. A twinkle-toed guy is tap-dancing on

the wooden porch of the main lodge. (Either that or he is attempting to stomp out a termite infestation with syncopated rhythm.)

I realize, despite what Ms. Sherron and Ms. O'Mara may believe, I have absolutely, positively no business being at Camp Footlights.

To make things worse, I quickly learn that a lot of the kids coming to my three-week session have already been up here for months, attending other three-week sessions.

"Hey, Jennifer!" shouts a guy (with very good diction).

"Hi, Joshua. Ready for another three weeks of drama camp drama?"

"You bet!"

It's August, remember? Turns out, some of these mega-talented young performers checked in back in June!

Cliques have formed. Friendships have been forged. Newbies need not apply for membership in either.

"Hey, new kid?" someone shouts. I think he might be a camp counselor. He's college-aged and wearing a Camp Footlights polo shirt, khaki shorts, and stretchy socks that climb up to his knees. All he needs is a whistle on a lanyard. He is, however, holding a clipboard—a sure sign of authority anywhere!

"Yes, sir?" I say.

"I'm Shawn. I have a theater degree. Almost. Drop your bag inside the lodge. You need to be at the auditions."

"Um, what auditions?"

Shawn gives me an eye roll and a sigh. "For next weekend's shows."

Right, I think. *The one my whole family is coming up to see.*

"Those are, like, right now?" I ask.

Shawn the counselor raises both eyebrows. I am soooooo wasting his time.

"No, they are not 'like' right now. They ARE right now!" He consults his clipboard. "Unfortunately, because you arrived later than we advised you to…"

"There was traffic."

"There's always traffic. Anyway, the only show that still has any openings is *Ashley!*"

"Like the name Ashley?"

"Exactly like the name Ashley. But with an exclamation point. Remind me of your name."

"I'm Jacky. Jacky Hart."

"Well, Jacky, up here the campers write, produce, and perform all the shows. It's what Mr. Beasley calls our total immersion experience. *Ashley!* was written by one of our true stars. Oh, who am I kidding? She's our biggest, brightest star: Ashley Jones! Mr. Beasley says she's destined to become the next Mariah Carey. No, even bigger. Ashley Jones is going to be *his* Latoya Sherron! Hurry. You might be able to land a role in the chorus."

"Where are the auditions?"

I earn another eye roll from Shawn. This guy is so exasperated with me. "In the barn theater, of course."

"Cool. And where's that?"

Now I get the *You are thicker than a slab of concrete* look.

"In the barn."

He points.

I take off running.

"Your luggage?" Shawn calls after me.

"Oh. Right. Thanks."

I grab my bag and haul it into the lodge, where another counselor tags it and slides it into a storage closet.

"Shouldn't you be at your audition?" she asks.

No, I think. *I should be back home in Seaside Heights.*

But that's not what I say.

"Thanks," I tell her. "I'm off to the barn for my first Camp Footlights cattle call."

I'm making a joke. Auditions with big groups of performers are sometimes known as cattle calls. And since this one is in a barn...

I get nothing.

Except another eye roll and disappointed head shake.

Oh, yeah. I'm really going to fit in here.

CHAPTER 14

S o, exactly how lost are you?" asks someone behind me.

I'm standing in the lobby of the Camp Footlights lodge, looking at all the different doors I could take, not knowing where any of them lead. I turn around.

There's a short, smiling girl behind me.

"I'm Brooklyn," she says. "From Brooklyn. No last name—I want to be a monomym like Madonna or Prince. And despite what you might be thinking, I am not short. I'm four feet, eleven and three-quarters inches tall. But on me, those three-quarters equal an inch and a half. You know that saying 'I'm all that and a bag of chips'?" She points at herself. "That was inspired by me."

"I'm Jacky," I say. "Jacky Hart."

"Nice to meet you, Jacky Hart. You're new here, right?"

I make a funny face and puff a hair-bobbing breath out of the corner of my mouth. "Is it that obvious?"

"Totes," says Brooklyn. "I'm a first-timer, too. But this is my second session."

"What's your talent?" I ask. "Singing? Dancing? Acting?"

Brooklyn shrugs. "Let me get back to you on that one, Jacky Hart. I'm what they call a work in progress. But, after three weeks of intensive training here at Camp Footlights, I'm pretty good at finding my way around. Where do you need to be?"

"The barn theater. I'm supposed to be at an audition for a show called *Ashley!* with an exclamation point."

"Oh," says Brooklyn with a wink. "An audition in a barn, eh? A genuine cattle call."

"Exactly!" I say, relieved to have finally found a kindred spirit. Someone whose mind works the way mine does.

"Come on," says Brooklyn. "I'll show you the way. Because you know what they say: There's no business like *show* business."

I groan a little and make a pained face.

"Yeah," says Brooklyn. "That one was definitely a groaner. Inside? I'm making a stinky face at myself."

We head out of the lodge and down a gravel path through a grove of pine trees.

"So, Jacky," says Brooklyn. "Where do you live?"

"I'm from Seaside Heights. That's in New Jersey."

Brooklyn nods. "That's okay. I won't hold it against you. I dig Jersey. Although I don't understand why they call it the Garden State. I've never seen very many tomatoes or cucumbers. Just oil refineries."

"That's only along the turnpike."

"Well, that's the only part I've ever seen. But all those smokestacks lined up in a tidy row? That kind of looks like a garden."

"So who's this Ashley Jones?"

"Oh, you'll find out soon enough."

"What's that supposed to mean?" I ask with a laugh.

Brooklyn wiggles both her eyebrows. "Oh, you'll find out soon enough."

CHAPTER 15

We reach a field and I see a big red barn.

Duh. Guess that's the barn theater. A man with a neatly trimmed beard, serious glasses, and wavy hair he probably loves to flick on a regular basis waddles out the front door. He's wearing a long-sleeve turtleneck and pleated pants even though it's the middle of August.

A woman in her twenties scurries behind him, carrying one of those notepad binder things. She's dressed in a smock. One hip pocket is embroidered with a tragedy face mask, the other a comedy face mask, proving she's serious about "the thee-ah-tuh," which is how you say *theater* when you're trying to be fancy, something I seldom try to be.

"That's Mr. Beasley," Brooklyn whispers. "Camp director."

"Who's that walking two feet behind him?" I whisper back.

"Echo."

"Huh?"

"Her real name is Rebecca something-or-other. She just graduated from NYU with a theater arts degree. We all just call her Echo."

"Why?"

Brooklyn gives me a sideways grin and, once again, says, "Oh, you'll find out soon enough."

"Brooklyn?" says Mr. Beasley when he sees us. He tilts back his head so he can look down his nose at her.

"Hey, Mr. Beasley."

"What on earth are you doing here?" he sniffs.

"What are you doing here?" mumbles his assistant, Smock Lady.

"Surely you're not auditioning for *Ashley with an Exclamation Point*?" says Mr. Beasley. I think he's what people call pompous, haughty, arrogant, or a twit. One of those.

"Surely not Ashley Exclamation Point," mumbles the assistant, who, okay, *echoes* everything her boss utters.

"No," says Brooklyn. "I mean, I wasn't planning on auditioning. Just trying to help out our newest camper. Jacky Hart. She needs a show to work in this week, and they say *Ashley!* is all that's left."

Now Mr. Beasley tilts back his head and looks down his nose at me. (He really should tweezer a few of his wirier nasal hairs. They don't exactly blend in with his curly mustache.)

"Oh, right," he says, eyeballing Brooklyn and then giving me a quick once-over. "You're Jacqueline Hart."

"Jacqueline Hart" is the echo.

"Guilty as charged," I say with my winningest smile. It's a real loser with Mr. Beasley.

He snickers a little. "We've been expecting you. Good luck with the audition. I'm sure Ashley will know exactly what to do with you."

His mumbling flunky, of course, echoes it.

"Ashley will know exactly what to do with *you*."

She even snickers.

The two of them remind me of Bubblebutt and Ringworm back in kindergarten—if only one of them did all the talking.

"While we're here, let's head downstairs to the costume shop, Rebecca," says the camp director. "Ashley's top hat needs to sizzle and sparkle in the spotlight. Michael needs to heat up his hot-glue gun. It's bling time!"

"Bling time," mumbles Echo.

They toddle off toward one of the barn's side doors. Yes, Echo even echoes Mr. Beasley's wobbly walk.

"And now you get to go inside and meet Ashley Jones," says Brooklyn. "This certainly is your lucky day, Jacky."

She's being sarcastic, of course.

And I have a feeling I'm gonna wish I never left the Garden State.

CHAPTER 16

O kay, people, settle down," says a very blond girl who moves like a gazelle onto the stage.

How does a gazelle move, you may wonder? Much more quickly and gracefully than me, that's for sure. The blond girl also has incredible teeth. First, they're all straight. Second, they shine. It's like she swallowed a chandelier filled with hundred-watt bulbs.

She claps her hands. "Find a seat. Sit down, people. There are audition forms and pencils on the cushions."

"But don't sit on the pencils," I whisper to Brooklyn.

"They might poke you in the butt," she whispers back.

"For those of you who don't know," the girl
announces, gliding back and forth across the stage,
strutting her stuff like a runway model, "I'm Ashley
Jones. You're here, of course, to audition for the
show I created, wrote, produced, scored, and will be
directing, choreographing, and starring in. It's called
Ashley with an Exclamation Point.

"I got the idea for my title from *Liza with a Z,* which, as you know, was a smash Broadway hit *and* movie starring Liza Minnelli, the fabulous daughter of the even more fabulous Judy Garland. It was directed and choreographed by the legendary Bob Fosse. If you didn't already know all of that, ask yourself a question: What are you doing here at Camp Footlights?"

Good question. The same one I keep asking myself. I guess I need to find out who this Bob Fosse guy is and why he's so legendary.

Everybody in the barn's auditorium applauds. No, they give Ashley a standing ovation. Brooklyn and I exchange a sideways glance but clap along anyhow. There's something about Ashley Jones. She has a very commanding stage presence. I bet she has it even when she's not onstage.

"So, aspiring thespians, singers, and dancers," Ashley says dramatically (which I'm guessing is how she says everything), "today I am looking for my supporting cast. That is, if you are cast in this show, *you* will support *me. Ashley with an Exclamation Point* is really a one-woman show with some other people in it. Mostly backup singers and background dancers.

I'll be the one doing all the work at center stage. Constantly. What's in this show for you?" She pauses to sparkle and blink. "Easy. This is your big chance to be onstage with me!"

More cheering from her adoring fans.

This time, Brooklyn and I just exchange a side-eye.

But if what that first camp counselor, the guy with the clipboard, told me is true, *Ashley with an Exclamation Point* is the only show that currently has any slots open in its cast. And my family's coming up next weekend to see me in...something. Anything.

"Specifically," Ashley goes on, "we have several openings for dogs in this very Paula Abdul–ish song-and-dance number I've created where, of course, I am Paula Abdul."

Now, kids, Paula Abdul—in case you don't remember her from that time she was a celebrity judge on *American Idol*—is a singer and dancer who started out on the Los Angeles Lakers cheerleading team when she was eighteen and later became their choreographer. After making up dance moves for Janet Jackson, she had one of the most successful debut albums of all time. It sold seven million copies! Anyway, in 1991, she's a huge star. And in her "Opposites Attract" video, she does a cool dance with a cartoon cat.

Sounds like Ashley wants to one-up Paula and dance with a pack of dogs.

So I dutifully fill out my form and wait my turn to be interviewed by Ashley. Brooklyn fills out a form, too.

"Right now, Ashley's the only game in town," she says with a shrug.

"There are no small parts, only small actors," I say, quoting something I picked up doing Shakespeare Down the Shore.

Brooklyn gives me a look and shakes her head.

"Nah," she says. "Not with Ashley Jones. With Ashley, there are *only* small parts and one ginormous star. Her!"

CHAPTER 17

I sit in the barn and wait for my audience with the queen.

Finally, she calls my name.

Somehow, she mispronounces it.

"Jacques-kay Hairt?" she says.

"Um, here." I raise my hand.

"You may approach." Ashley beckons for me to come onstage.

"It's Jacky Hart," I tell her after I climb up the steps and join her in the blazingly bright spotlight that seems to follow her everywhere.

"What's Jacky Hart?" she asks.

"My name. You pronounced it Jacques-kay Hairt."

"You're new here, aren't you?"

"Yes?"

"Here's a tip, Jacky Hart. To be in the chorus of a show, you have to be a team player. You can't complain about every little thing. If you do, you'll quickly get a reputation as a diva."

"What's a diva?"

"Someone who is very demanding and difficult to work with."

O-kay, I think. *Guess I won't demand that this diva pronounce my name correctly.*

She glances at my audition form, where I've listed some of the shows I've done.

She breezes through them. *"A Midsummer Night's Dream, You Can't Take It with You, You're a Good Man, Charlie Brown."* She pauses. "Who'd you play in *Charlie Brown*?"

"Snoopy," I say. "The dog."

She eye-rolls me. "I know who and what Snoopy is! So you have experience doing doggy moves?"

"Yeah. Everybody said I was—"

She shows me her palm. "Sorry. Not really interested. There is just soooo much to think about when you're writing, producing, and starring in a one-woman show. Really can't waste too many brain cells on other stuff, know what I mean? Okay, show me what you've got." She snaps her fingers and taps her toes to give me a beat. "Five, six, seven, eight!"

I do my Snoopy dance from *You're a Good Man, Charlie Brown*. To be honest, I could've done anything. Ashley isn't even watching me. I notice a full-length mirror in the front row of the auditorium. That's where Ashley's looking. At her own reflection. She's striking all sorts of puckered-lip poses. The girl was doing selfies long before camera phones were invented.

"Fantastic!" says Ashley after I flail around for about a minute. I think she's talking about her final pouty pose.

I take it as my cue to stop dancing.

"Here." Ashley hands me some sheet music. "You're fine. You can be one of the dogs who loves me, but I keep shooing you away because, like the song says, 'My Best Friend Is Me.' I wrote the lyrics. Go change into your dance clothes. Call time for our first rehearsal is two. Don't be late. If you are, you'll be cut from the cast."

"Okay," I say. "Thanks."

Ashley doesn't say, *You're welcome*. She just shoos me away with a flick of her very nicely manicured hand. I descend from the stage and almost take a tumble on the steps because that spotlight Ashley lives in? It can really blind ya.

"Next?" says Ashley, putting a hand over her eyes so she can scout out the auditorium seats. "Is that you, Brooklyn?"

"Yeah," says my new friend.

"Well, this certainly is a surprise. I wasn't expecting to see you."

"I'm not one hundred percent sure I want to audition," says Brooklyn, hiding her filled-in form behind her back.

Ashley rolls her eyes in exasperation. "Such a prima donna. Fine, Brooklyn. Fine. You don't need to audition. I know your work from the last session. You can be in the dog chorus, too."

"Gee, thanks."

"Don't mention it."

Brooklyn turns to me. "Let's go get you unpacked. It's already noon. Guess we need to be back here in two hours."

"I didn't bring any dance clothes," I say, feeling slightly embarrassed.

"Do you have sweatpants?"

"Yeah."

"Sweatpants will work. They're loose. You can move in 'em. Come on."

We head back to the lodge by a different route. There's a sidewalk with stars set into the concrete. Famous former camper names are inscribed on the stars. I see Caroline Jean Risvold, the mega movie star. Latoya Sherron's star is cemented into the next square.

"That is so cool," I say. "Just think, all these famous people walked the same path we're walking right now!"

"I guess," says Brooklyn with another one of her nonchalant shrugs. "I don't really go gaga for showbiz celebrities."

"Really? But this is a showbiz camp."

"I know. But I prefer scientists."

"Seriously?"

"Oh, yeah. Scientists don't play make-believe, Jacky. They actually *do* something. Come on. Room two-thirty-five is in the west wing of the lodge."

"Is, uh, that my room?" I ask.

"Yep."

"And you know this because...?"

"Easy," says Brooklyn. "We're roommates!"

CHAPTER 18

Brooklyn and I skip lunch.

I really don't want to go to my first rehearsal on a full stomach, because I don't want to repeat my barf-a-thon performance from the boardwalk.

A little before two, as we walk back to the barn theater, Brooklyn gives me what we used to call the 411 (because that's the number we'd call for information) on Ashley Jones.

"This is her sixth summer at Camp Footlights. She's Mr. Beasley's favorite. Madame Lamond's, too."

"Who's Madame Lamond?" I wonder.

"The camp's top dance instructor. Madame Lamond is going to help Ashley with the choreography on her show, even though Ashley will take all the credit for it."

"So we're really going to have to d-d-dance?"

Brooklyn nods. "I'm afraid that's what chorus kids do. They sing. They dance. And they do both in the background."

I nod. I, of course, know this.

"How far b-b-back do you th-th-think we can go?"

Brooklyn stops walking. There's a worried expression on her face. She puts both her hands on my shoulders and looks me in the eye. "Are you okay, Jacky?"

"Y-y-yeah. I s-s-sometimes stutter when I get n-n-nervous."

She smiles and winks. "Well, stick with me. We'll bumble through the moves together—way back in the background. Because I can't dance, either."

"You can't?"

"That's right. Check your stereotypes at the door, people. I can't dance, I can't sing, and I can't dunk. Plus, like I said, I dig scientists. They're my rock stars."

I think Brooklyn is saying all this to make me feel better.

And guess what? It's working.

When we enter the barn theater, Madame Lamond is already there, scowling at us and looking very stern. She reminds me of a ballet instructor who just stepped out of a Degas oil painting. Not that she has brushstrokes all over her face or anything. She just looks like she might be French and that she definitely means business. She has one of those walking sticks ballet teachers sometimes use to point with. Or maybe they use them to poke and prod their dancers. Maybe to play billiards. Like I said, I'm not really a dancer.

Ashley already has her moves memorized. She leaps and shimmies and arm-swings her way across the stage.

"You are perfection in motion, my dear," Madame Lamond gushes as Ashley gracefully bounds, twirls, swirls, taps, kicks, and time-steps through her big number. While she's moving, she's singing the song she'll be singing to us, her backup dogs:

"Sorry, pooch, you just have to see,
This is how it's gotta be.
Don't go barking up my tree.

My best friend is me-ee.
My best friend is ME!"

"Such powerful lyrics, Ashley!" raves Madame Lamond in her thick French accent, which makes her words sound even more gushy. *"Mon Dieu!* And accompanied by such powerful yet graceful movement? You, Ashley, are my gazelle."

See? I was right about the girl's gazelle-ish-ness.

Madame Lamond taps her walking stick on the stage's wooden floor. "Chorus? It is now your turn. Please form three lines behind our star."

Most of the kids race to be in the front line. Brooklyn and I shamble to the back.

Then Madame Lamond gives us our steps.

"It's a very simple combination," she says. "Riffle, riffle, right, right. Fan kick, fan kick, left, left. Heel ball change, heel ball change, jazz hands, jazz hands. Heel toe, heel toe, cakewalk, scoot, scoot. Then, of course, the big finish: hand spin, head spin, pop, pop, spin!"

She might as well be speaking French.

"And here we go. Five, six, seven, eight. Riffle, riffle, right, right. Fan kick, fan kick, left, left."

This rehearsal feels too much like gym class or football practice. There are too many rigid rules. Too many pre-planned steps. (Although, to be fair, I think that's why they call it choreography.)

Frustrated, bumbling around, and out of step with everybody else on the stage, I decide to make up my own dance. I flap my legs, flail my arms, do the twist to the right and the twist to the left. Then I twist again. I do the swim, the mashed potato, and the funky chicken. I even throw in a few moves from

that movie *Footloose*. I'm doing my best to make people laugh with my comedic ballet.

Remember how I said I'm a bad influence on my younger sister Riley? I'm having the same effect on Brooklyn.

She thinks what I'm doing is hysterical. So she joins in and mirrors my moves.

Madame Lamond is not amused.

She bangs that stick on the floor. The music screeches to a halt. Ashley stops singing.

"You two!" barks the camp's top dance instructor. "In the back line. Do you think this is some kind of joke?"

Well, I want to say, *folks back home* do *call me Jacky Ha-Ha*.

But I don't. I just drop my head and look down at my feet.

Now Madame Lamond gasps.

"Brooklyn?"

Brooklyn gives the dance instructor a wiggly finger wave. "Hey there, Madame Lamond."

"Are those two trying to upstage me?" demands Ashley.

"Oui," says Madame Lamond. "It appears they are."

"They're not true musical comedy material, Madame Lamond!" shrieks Ashley. Then she stomps offstage in a tizzy.

Madame Lamond turns to Brooklyn. "I am very disappointed seeing you behave this way. I will assume that this new girl, this class clown, is a bad influence."

"Nah. She's just Jacky. She's my new friend and roomie."

"Report to the costume shop immediately!" fumes Madame Lamond. "Both of you! There, you will neither sing nor dance. There, all you will do is sit and sew!"

CHAPTER 19

So, yeah—Brooklyn and I are basically banished to the basement of the barn.

The costume shop.

It's a dark, cinderblock-walled room. There are a couple of sewing machines, bolts of fabric on tables, mannequins with costume fragments pinned to their torsos. Through the ceiling, we can hear all the dancers clomping across the stage, which is directly above us. The show must go on. Even if Brooklyn and I must not go on with it.

"I'm sorry," I tell Brooklyn.

"For what?" she says. "I had a blast. That dance was the bomb! As far as I'm concerned, Madame Lamond can take that stick of hers and—"

"Brooklyn?"

A boy a few years older than us steps out of a door labeled COSTUME STORAGE. He's hugging a lumpy bundle of star-spangled somethings.

"Hey, Michael," says Brooklyn.

"What are you doing down here?"

She gestures at me. "We're your new costume assistants. This is my friend Jacky Hart. She's wicked funny."

"Uh, hi," I say.

I feel like I should shake hands with Michael, but he has that bundle of sequined costumes in his arms. Speaking of his arms, they kind of ripple with muscles. Not that I was, you know, noticing his muscles or their ripples. Or his cute face. Didn't notice any of that at all.

"Hi," he says softly. Michael is extremely handsome, with feathery, swept-back hair. Okay, the hair I noticed. He could be on the cover of *Teen Beat* magazine.

He sets the costumes down on a cutting table.

"So," he says, "who'd you offend to wind up down here?"

"Queen Ashley," says Brooklyn. "And Madame Lamond."

"Oooh. A double-header."

"It was kind of my fault," I say. "I was goofing around. Making up my own dance."

Michael arches an eyebrow. "I take it you dance to the beat of a different drummer?"

"Yep," I say.

"Don't we all?" says Brooklyn.

"Well," I say, "my different drummer isn't even in the band. They make him play outside on overturned plastic paint tubs. Anyway, I got us both kicked out of *Ashley with an Exclamation Point*."

Now Michael rolls his eyes. "You're not the first. Probably won't be the last."

"So how can we help down here?" asks Brooklyn.

"Well, I pulled all the blingy coats we have in storage. Hopefully one will be sparkly enough for Ashley. Mr. Beasley wants her to 'shine like the star she is.' We'll worry about whether it fits later. Now we need to find her a top hat. A glittery top hat. Think *A Chorus Line*, big finale, singular sensation sparkly."

"Got it," says Brooklyn.

"Got it," I say, even though I don't really know
what Michael is talking about. I think it's some
more of that theater kid code I need to catch up on.

Brooklyn and I follow Michael into the dimly
lit costume storage area on our quest for spangly
top hats. We walk through a wardrobe warehouse
in what feels like the catacombs beneath the barn
theater's auditorium. It's a giant closet filled with

costumes from past shows, all patiently waiting for their next entrance. Shelves above the clothing racks are lined with cardboard boxes and plastic bins.

"Oh, my," says Michael, rummaging through some clothes in a section labeled OLIVER!

He pulls out a hanger with a tattered tunic, some knee-high britches, and a rumpled cotton shirt. There is a floppy hat looped through the hanger hook.

"This was my costume!" he gushes. "From six years ago when we did *Oliver!*"

"Who'd you play?" I ask.

Michael blushes a little. "Oliver," he says. Then he quickly jams the hanger back in its spot.

"You were the lead?" I say.

"I guess," says Michael.

"You've been coming here since you were ten, right?" says Brooklyn.

"Yuh-huh. Camp Footlights? These are my people." He points to a section of racks up ahead. "The *Chorus Line* top hats are in those boxes on the third shelf."

Brooklyn pulls over a platform ladder.

Michael scampers up it.

"So what show are you in this weekend?" I innocently ask.

"None of them," says Michael.

"But you used to? You were in *Oliver!*..."

"Yes, Jacky. I *used* to be in shows. Not anymore."

"What happened?" I wonder.

Michael turns around and gives me a look. "Ashley Jones."

CHAPTER 20

T he next day is Sunday, and nobody is going to rehearsals for *Ashley!* or prepping for any of the other shows in that week's showcase.

We're all boarding a bus for New York City!

We've been invited to a matinee preview of *Birds of a Feather*, a Broadway musical starring, drum-roll please, Latoya Sherron! That's right—when Ms. Sherron came to see me down the shore, it was on her day off from rehearsals for what's sure to be her next big Broadway smash.

I am totally stoked about the trip down to the city.

Brooklyn? Not so much.

"I'm going to hang out in the costume shop," she tells us over breakfast.

"Why?" says Michael, who's eating at our table. "I'm not going to be down there, and I'm in charge of costumes this summer. I wouldn't miss Latoya Sherron in anything. She's a goddess."

Brooklyn shrugs. "We have to hot-glue sequins on all those dog collars."

Yes, it's true. Ashley wants her backup dancer dogs to be spangly, too. "They should glisten behind me like twinkling stars" were the instructions on the note she had delivered to the costume shop. It was written with swirling purple ink on frilly pink paper. "The twinkling stars from a galaxy far, far away, of course. None of them should sparkle brighter than me!"

"Are you sure?" I say to Brooklyn.

"I'm positive," she says. "But you two? Go! Enjoy!"

Of course, I don't let on that I know Latoya Sherron. That she's my sponsor, my "patron of the arts," as they used to say back in the Renaissance. In other words, I don't tell people Ms. Sherron is footing the bill for my stay at Camp Footlights. I want to keep that kind of thing a secret. Not that I'm embarrassed to be receiving her financial aid. Okay. I am. Totally. But I also don't want people to think I'm bragging or name-dropping. *Oh, yes, I know the star of this Broadway show. What Broadway stars do you know?*

On the bus ride down to New York City, Michael and I (unfortunately) wind up in the seat right behind Mr. Beasley and Echo. Mr. Beasley spends a lot of time finger-twirling the hair behind his left ear and whining about the show we're going to see.

"I wish we were seeing *Phantom* or *The Secret Garden*," he says.

"Phantom's secret garden," mutters Echo.

"Even *The Will Rogers Follies* would be better."

"Rogers Will Follies better" is the echo.

Mr. Beasley sighs. "But I suppose we can't beat the ticket price for this Latoya Sherron show."

"But can't beat Latoya ticket."

"It's free."

Echo nods before she mutters, "Free."

As we approach Times Square and the Theater District, I can't believe my eyes. I've never been in Manhattan before. There are so many people on the streets. So many shows. So many carts that smell like charcoal where vendors sell hot dogs and pretzels and knishes. So many bright lights bedazzling the marquees outside all the Broadway theaters.

"Wow!" is all I can say as I step off the bus and twirl around, trying to take it all in. "Wow, wow, wow, wow, wow!"

Michael snaps a photo of me standing in front of the Music Box Theatre, where *Birds of a Feather* is playing. Over my shoulder looms a huge illuminated picture of Latoya Sherron smiling down at me!

I know her! I want to shout. *I did a show with her!*

But I don't. Ashley Jones is giving me a look that

says I'm acting like a rube. A hick from the sticks. I guess you're supposed to act cool and aloof even when you're about to see your VERY FIRST BROADWAY SHOW EVER! Even when it stars somebody YOU ACTUALLY KNOW.

Mr. Beasley sees my big smile and shakes his head.

"Too bad *you'll* never perform on the Great White Way, Miss Hart," he says.

"Too bad never," says Echo, shaking her head.

Mr. Beasley gives me one of his haughty sniffs. "From what I hear, you're just not musical comedy material."

Echo nods. "NMCM."

I assume they've been talking to Madame Lamond. And Ashley. And everybody else who saw my improvised modern dance routine.

It might've been comical (to me and Brooklyn, anyway).

But I guess it wasn't very Broadway musical–ish.

CHAPTER 21

The show blows me away.

It's funny. It's peppy. It tugs at my heart and gives me goose bumps.

All of a sudden, I don't care what Mr. Beasley says, even if his flunky, Echo, repeats it.

I want to be on Broadway someday.

As I watch Latoya Sherron work her amazing magic, it's *all* I want to do. I can see myself onstage, basking in the love of the audience, just like she's doing so graciously every time she finishes another incredible number.

Only, I won't be dancing. And probably not singing.

But I'd be the one with the bit part getting all the laughs!

Just like Suzanne Brooks. She has only two scenes in the first act of *Birds of a Feather*. She doesn't sing a note. But Suzanne Brooks stole both those scenes because she's hysterical. And her comic timing? Amazing. She also knows how to do a perfect pratfall. (By the way, *pratfall* is a polite way of saying you land on your butt.)

Intermission comes too quickly.

"If you didn't use the bathroom before the show started," Ashley informs our camp group, "good luck. The bathrooms in Broadway theaters are notoriously teeny-tiny. The line for the ladies' room will be impossible. Next time, do like Mr. Beasley and I did. Go before the show."

"What Ashley says is true," says Mr. Beasley. "Go *before* the show!"

"So true," adds Echo. "Before the show, go, go, go!"

"But that's why you kids come to camp," says Mr. Beasley. "To learn everything there is to learn about show business from professionals such as myself."

Thankfully, Echo goes with a shorter version of the speech. "Why you camp pro fish for my elf."

Unfortunately, I need to brave that ladies' room line. I had an orange drink before the curtain went up. Michael said Broadway theaters were famous for their orange drinks, so I had to try one.

Now I must pay the price.

The line for the ladies' room is, as advertised, extremely long.

But Ms. O'Mara is in it!

"Jacky?" She sees me before I see her.

"Hi!"

"Are you here with the Camp Footlights kids?"

"Yep. It's my first Broadway show!"

"Isn't Latoya amazing?"

"Incredible."

"I'm going backstage after the curtain call," my favorite teacher in the whole world says. "Want to come with me? I'm sure Latoya would love to see you."

"I'd love to see her, too. But I'm with everybody else. We have a bus."

"It can wait five minutes. All the Broadway shows let out at the same time. The streets get so congested, it's impossible to drive anywhere anyhow."

"I don't know...."

"I'll talk to the camp director. What's his name? Weasley?"

I laugh. "Mr. Beasley. But, to tell the truth, he's also a little weaselly."

We both visit the ladies' room. Somehow, the Broadway ushers make it work. They get everybody in and out with enough time left over to buy another orange drink (which I don't do).

Ms. O'Mara has a word with Mr. Beasley.

He reluctantly agrees to wait for me to say hello to Ms. Sherron after the show.

"You'll have five minutes," he tells me.

"Five minutes you'll have," comes the echo.

The second act is even better than the first. Ms. Sherron has a big number near the end that blows the roof off the theater. Not really. There was no actual damage done to the theater's ceiling or roof. But her song is a real showstopper, meaning they have to stop the show so Ms. Sherron can bask in the adulation of a standing ovation before the performance even ends!

Oh, and Suzanne Brooks is hysterical in her second-act scenes. She steals all three of them. She's who I want to be when I grow up.

After the final curtain, Ms. O'Mara takes me backstage to the star's dressing room. By the way, it's amazing. There are so many bouquets lined up on the counters. So many lightbulbs ringing the mirrors. So many notes from well-wishers.

"Hey, Jacky," says Ms. Sherron.

For an instant, I can't believe it. The Broadway star who just took all those bows actually knows my name.

"You were amazing!" I say when I remember how to speak.

"Thanks," she says.

"Oh, can I have your autograph?" I ask.

Ms. O'Mara and Ms. Sherron both stare at me a little when I make the slightly odd request. Ms. Sherron signed all sorts of stuff for me when we did that Shakespeare show together in Seaside Heights.

"Um, sure," says Ms. Sherron, probably thinking I'm greedy.

"It's not for me. It's for my new friend Michael."

"Ohhh," says Ms. Sherron, smiling and nodding. "A fellow camper?"

"Yeah."

"So how are things going up at Camp Footlights?"

"Pretty good. Thank you again for setting it all up and, well, for everything!"

"My pleasure. How's your roommate?"

"Brooklyn? She's great. That's her name. Brooklyn. She was born in Brooklyn."

Ms. Sherron nods. "Interesting."

"She doesn't have a last name," I explain. "Well, she probably has one, but she doesn't use it. She's like Madonna or Prince. One name only."

"And this Brooklyn is a good kid?" asks Ms. Sherron.

"Oh, yeah. We're already besties."

"That's great news. My roommate at Camp Footlights? All she did was snore."

CHAPTER 22

Monday afternoon (after a few fun acting classes that, woo-hoo, Ashley wasn't in), I'm ready to head back to the costume shop so I can hot-glue some more sequins.

Brooklyn doesn't come with me. "I have this thing I have to take care of," she tells me.

"What kind of thing?" I ask.

"The important kind" is the only answer I get. But Brooklyn does wink, so that makes me think it's something personal. And secret. Maybe even a boy-girl thing? My big sister Sophia would be so proud.

I shoot Brooklyn a thumbs-up to let her know *I get it.*

She goes her way. I go mine.

Down in the costume shop, Michael has already framed and hung his Latoya Sherron autograph right over his sewing machine.

"I can't believe you actually know Latoya Sherron!" he says with a hand to his heart.

"I played one of the fairies in a production of *A Midsummer Night's Dream* that she starred in back home. Because she knows my teacher, Ms. O'Mara. They did *Annie* together when they were kids."

The more shows I mention, the more I remember how I'm not going to be in one this weekend and how my whole family is driving up from Jersey to see me in a show, which, like I just said, I won't be in!

While I'm stressing, Michael is beaming. "I will cherish this autograph always. I will also take it with me wherever I go, except, you know, not to the bathroom or anything."

"Riiiiight. Good call."

"So where's Brooklyn?" he asks.

"I'm not sure."

"I really could've used her help today...."

"What's up?"

"Brandon Maloney."

"Who's that?"

"This genius ten-year-old writer."

Seriously? You can be a genius when you're ten?

"He reminds me of that comedian Jerry Seinfeld," says Michael. "You know—the guy with that TV show."

"Seinfeld's funny," I say.

"So's Brandon. I mean, he writes funny. But he always acts like the sky is falling. Plus, Ashley has declared that Brandon, like me, is not true musical comedy material."

"That's what she said about me, too."

"Welcome to the club. Anyway, we're in a real costume crunch because Brandon came up with a goofy last-minute show idea for this Saturday's showcase. I guess it's more a sketch or a skit than a full-blown play." Michael gestures to a table with what look like giant white pillowcases and sheets of felt—yellow, orange, red, brown. "It sounds like a hoot. He calls it *Scrambled Egg*. It's all about an egg that doesn't want to get tossed into a frying pan with two sizzling strips of very angry bacon."

I'm laughing because one of the acting exercises in my early-morning class was to "be" a strip of bacon sputtering and shrinking in a pan. Not sure what the point of it was, but it was fun.

"The costumes are pretty simple," says Michael. "But I could use help. Especially since we still need to add more sparkles to Ashley's top hat. The girl has high bling expectations."

"I'll take care of the hat," I say. "You whip up the eggs and bacon."

"Perfect."

About an hour later, we're both working away on our projects when this short kid with long hair ambles into the costume shop.

"I'm dead, Michael!" he says, throwing both his hands up. "Dead, I tell you!"

Michael rolls his eyes. "Having a bad day, Brandon?"

"Yeah, someone stole my mood ring. I don't know how I feel about that." He looks at the two bacon costumes Michael's laid out on a cutting table. "Will these shrink when you wash them or only when you fry them? You know, doctors say that each strip of bacon you eat takes nine minutes off your life. I should've died in 1492."

I'm shaking my head and laughing. The little kid is funny.

"So what's the problem?" Michael asks Brandon.

"My egg quit!" Brandon exclaims. "She wanted to sing and dance and become the next Ashley Jones. I told her not everything in the theater is singing and dancing or Ashley Jones. She told me to grow up. I told her, 'I'm ten. I'm working on it!'"

Brandon shakes his shaggy head.

"I blame Mr. Beasley. In my humble—make that *expert*—opinion, the man has ruined Camp Footlights. He wants to turn us into a branch of the Beef 'n' Boards Dinner Theater, where he is the artistic—and I use that term loosely—director! Can you imagine? People eating prime rib and baked potatoes while actors perform onstage? Do they think it's a movie? Movie actors can't hear you chewing or asking for extra sour cream and bacon bits. Stage actors can! Plus, you can't get prime rib at the movie theater concession stand."

Michael laughs. "That'd be funny. A movie theater selling prime rib and baked potatoes along with the popcorn and candy."

"I need a new egg, Michael!" says Brandon, clutching his hands together to beg for divine intervention. "I need a new egg!"

I need to be in a show this weekend.

Any show.

I raise my hand. "I'll do it."

CHAPTER 23

Okay, playing an egg in a wacky sketch with two slabs of bacon won't be the same as doing Shakespeare Down the Shore or starring as Snoopy in *You're a Good Man, Charlie Brown.*

But my whole family is coming up to see me in a show on Saturday, and right now, playing the lead character in *Scrambled Egg* sure beats sitting in the audience and showing off all the rhinestones I've glued into place this week for Ashley's costumes.

Besides, there's something about Brandon's weird, if somewhat dark, sense of humor that I like. The kid makes me laugh.

"Jacky here is hilarious," Michael tells Brandon. "Back home in Jersey, they call her Jacky Ha-Ha."

"Yep," I say, mugging a funny face. "That's me. I'm like that Barbra Streisand movie. I'm a funny girl."

"Which was a Broadway show before it was a movie," says Michael, because, hey, he's a theater kid. They know their history.

Brandon pitches me the concept for his show. "It's a satirical take on what it means to be truly committed. To take a leap of faith into the great unknown."

I nod like I get all that thematic subtext stuff.

But, to tell the truth, I just want to know what the egg does. What's my comic bit? My schtick? And do I get to do a funny pratfall like Suzanne Brooks did in *Birds of a Feather*? Do I crack a few corny egg jokes or is the yolk on me?

Sorry. Couldn't resist.

"The two miserable strips of bacon are sizzling in the pan," says Brandon, holding up his hands to make a frame and picture the scene. "The pan is a trampoline. An egg rolls along, climbs a ladder, and, after some yuks, jumps into the frying pan with them."

Yes! I can do a pratfall.

"I'm in!" I tell Brandon.

"Great! Give Michael your measurements so he can make your costume."

"It's a baggy white sack with a yellow felt circle in the center," Michael explains. "No measurements required, Brandon."

"Fantastic!" says Brandon, looking sunnier than he did when he came into the costume shop. "Let me talk to my bacon strips. Work out a rehearsal schedule. You're in the lodge?"

I nod. "Jacky Hart. Room two-thirty-five."

"Cool. I'll slip the schedule under the door."

"Cool."

We shake hands, then Brandon dashes off.

"I'm in a show!" I say to Michael when the ten-year-old wunderkind is gone. "My parents will actually get to see me do something onstage!"

"It'll be a hoot. Can't wait to see you in that egg costume."

I hold up the top hat I've been working on. "I think this is done. There's not enough space on it for one more rhinestone, bangle, or bauble."

"Can you run it upstairs to Ashley?" He nods toward the ceiling. Once again, we are being serenaded by the stomping of feet from above. "I want to cut your yolk out of the yellow felt. Finish up these two bacon suits."

"No problem."

I slide the shimmering top hat into a round box and bound up the stairs to the stage. I can hear the music and Ashley belting out the "My Best Friend Is Me" song.

I also hear Madame Lamond counting out the steps for her dancers.

"And right, and right, and turn, turn, turn. Step left, step left, kick ball change, kick ball change."

I come up in the wings of the stage, where it's dark. My eyes slowly adjust as I wait for a break in the rehearsal. You really don't want to interrupt everybody just to deliver a hat, no matter how amazingly sparkly it is.

Ashley is in the spotlight at center stage, but my eye is quickly drawn to one of the background dog dancers.

Whoa, she is amazing. Like Latoya Sherron spectacular. Whoever the girl is, she definitely moves better than Ashley, which means Ashley probably hasn't seen her doing it yet, because the last thing Camp Footlights' resident superstar wants is someone upstaging her in the chorus.

Now the girl does a very balletic spin and

starts moonwalk-gliding away from me.

She slips into the spotlight beam behind Ashley.

I can see the girl's face.

It's Brooklyn!

Brooklyn told me she couldn't dance, sing, or dunk.

Huh.

Apparently, she was lying about at least one of those.

Go, Brooklyn!
Go, Brooklyn!

CHAPTER 24

T
ake five, everybody!" cries Ashley as someone
rushes onstage with a towel so she can dab the
sweat off her brow.

She sees me waiting in the wings.

"What are you gawking at?"

Yes, my chin is still halfway down my neck.
Because I'm staring stupidly at Brooklyn, who hasn't
seen me lurking in the shadowy wings, holding a
hatbox.

"Is that my hat?" says Ashley. "Gimme, gimme."
She makes the accompanying *Gimme-gimme* hand
gesture.

I march out to center stage and hand her the box.
Ashley pulls out the hat and blinks, repeatedly. She
is blinded by the bling.

"It's perfect!" she proclaims. "Congratulations, Jack Keyhart. It seems you've finally found your talent. Making hats. For *moi!*"

I mumble, "You're welcome," and drift over to where Brooklyn is toweling off her face.

"Brooklyn?"

She whips around. There is a look of panic plus guilt in her eyes.

"I can explain," she says.

I bow slightly, extending my right hand. "Yes, kindly do."

"Madame Lamond called my mother. My mother called me." She shrugs. "So here I am."

"This is the thing you had to take care of?"

"Yeah. Sorry."

"But you told me you couldn't dance."

She bites her lower lip. "Yeah. About that..."

I give her another sarcastic bow. "Please. Do go on."

"I was trying to make you feel better."

"Excuse me?"

"You were all, 'I can't dance.' Then you started stuttering. So I, you know, played along. Pretended I was a terrible dancer, too."

"Oh, so now I'm terrible?"

"No. You're funny. You just can't dance."

"Oh, I see. I'm so supernaturally *un*talented, I needed your pity."

"I didn't say that."

"You didn't have to. Actions speak louder than words. Unless, you know, you're screaming the words. Screamed words can be a lot louder than some actions, especially the quiet ones like, I don't know, petting a cat. That's not very loud, unless the cat starts purring."

Brooklyn's smiling. "You're very funny, Jacky."

"Am I? Or am I just really hurt right now so I'm very blabby and gabby? Enjoy the rest of your rehearsal. Don't let Ashley see how good you are. Maybe tell her you can't dance. It worked on me. Excuse me. I have to go try on an egg costume."

I storm off the stage.

This is the last thing I need. My first friend at Camp Footlights lied to me. Worse, she did it because she felt sorry for me.

Well, I don't need Brooklyn feeling sorry for me.

I know how to feel sorry for myself. I have a lot

of practice doing it. In some ways, it's my own one-woman show.

That night, I skip dinner and head down to a picnic table near the lake.

I don't want to be in the room with Brooklyn. I did grab a piece of Camp Footlights stationery out of the tiny desk we're supposed to share so I can write my mother a letter. It's something I did a lot when Mom was over in Saudi Arabia during the Gulf War.

I don't know if I'll ever send her this letter, but it always makes me feel better to write down my emotions.

I've been lying to myself. Being a performer is not who I was meant to be. If it were, God might've given me a little more talent. The kids up here at Camp Footlights? They're all superstars, Mom. They can sing, they can dance, they can act, they can probably even juggle while they walk on stilts. It's time for me to face facts. I don't fit in. Not in Seaside

Heights. Not at performing arts camp. Not anywhere. I wish I liked math more. I think I want to be an accountant when I grow up. Numbers don't lie to you. Numbers don't tell you they can't dance when they really can. Numbers don't need a spangly hat like something out of the Grand Ole Opry!

I fill the page.

And then I wad up the sheet of paper and toss it into a trash bin.

I do not feel better.

I need to do something bigger. Bolder. I need to climb a Ferris wheel and howl at the moon.

Unfortunately, there are no Ferris wheels at Camp Footlights.

But there is a full moon rising over the lake.

And the lake is surrounded by trees. Very tall trees. Some of them are even taller than the Ferris wheel back home in Seaside Heights. They might be easier to climb, too.

So that's where I am going to do my howling!

I clamber up the branches of a sturdy oak. I'm about forty feet off the ground. The moon is so big, it feels like I could reach out and poke that Mr. Man in the Moon right in one of his eyes.

I howl!

Yes, I feel better.

Until I look down.

Two branches below me, I see a very creepy raccoon sticking its head out of a big knothole. It's rubbing its paws together and smiling up at me with spooky moon-glow-reflector eyes.

I don't think it's going to let me climb down as easily as I climbed up.

I don't think it's going to let me climb down at all.

CHAPTER 25

Being trapped up a tree gives me time to think.

For instance, raccoons. What do they like to eat? Are my toes on the list? And why do they have to have such incredibly human faces? I have enough people giving me the stink eye. I don't need a furry garbage-can grazer glaring at me, too.

When I was up at the top of the Ferris wheel back home, I made a solemn vow with the stars, the ocean, and God as my witness. I promised that I would stop doing outrageous stuff (like climbing Ferris wheels) and fulfill my "tremendous potential," the one my teachers were always telling me I was wasting.

Well, in this tree, I make a vow before the moon, the raccoon, and God, if He or She's still listening to anything I solemnly vow, to quit worrying so much about what other people think about me. The answer to all of life's questions was written on that T-shirt flapping in the breeze back on the boardwalk: "Be yourself, Jacky. Everyone else is already taken."

So I'm going to do that.

Starting now. Right away. Okay, right after I get out of this tree.

"Jacky?" I hear a voice.

I hope it's not the raccoon. And if it is, I hope I wake up in a cartoon.

"Jacky!"

I look down.

Brooklyn is standing at the base of the tree. Michael is there with her. One of them has a flashlight and is swinging it around. Finally, it hits me. Yes, for the first time at Camp Footlights, I am the one the spotlight is aiming for.

"Uh, hi, guys," I say.

"Are you okay?" asks Michael. He has his hands cupped around his mouth to make a megaphone. I'm pretty high up.

"Yeah. But I'm afraid Rocky Raccoon down there might think I'm more than okay. He might think I'm magically delicious."

The spotlight lowers. Now the raccoon is center stage. It hisses. Maybe that's how raccoons sing show tunes.

"How'd you know where to find me?" I ask.

"We didn't!" says Michael.

"So we looked everywhere!" says Brooklyn.

"The flashlight picked up some glitter on that picnic table over there!" adds Michael.

Ha! If you spend your day sprinkling glitter flakes and hot-gluing sequins, you're always going to take some of your work home with you.

"Jacky?" shouts Brooklyn. "I'm sorry I lied about being a dancer."

"I should be the one apologizing to you," I shout back down. "A dancer is who you are, Brooklyn. It's who you were meant to be. Don't forget, I saw you dance. You're amazing."

"And you're hilarious!" she screams up at me.

"So maybe we should both just be who we're meant to be!" I yell.

"Works for me!" roars Brooklyn.

Yes, in the history of friends making up after an argument, I don't think one has ever been quite as loud as ours. Even the raccoon looks like it wants to cover its ears with its creepy little hands.

CHAPTER 26

"C an you climb down?" Michael calls out at the top
of his voice.

"Um, not really."

"We should call for help," says Brooklyn.

"On it," says Michael. He runs back to the lodge
to call whoever you call when a kid is stuck in a tree.
Probably the same people who deal with treed cats,
I'm thinking.

"So," I say to Brooklyn, "is that why Madame
Lamond was so upset with you when you joined me
in my goofy dance? She knows how good you actually are."

"Yeah. I guess. But, Jacky?"

"Yeah?"

"The goofy dance was fun. Who says choreography has to be serious all the time?"

"There was some funny dancing in *Birds of a Feather.*"

"Really?"

"Yeah. I wish you'd come to Broadway with us."

"Maybe next time."

"Yeah. Next time."

While we wait for the rescue squad, Brooklyn and I chat about all sorts of stuff. We decide that, maybe, one day, we'll do a show together. She'll do the beautiful dances; I'll do the funny schtick. Thirty minutes later, Michael leads some very friendly volunteer firefighters to my tree. They have an extremely long ladder.

They're joined down below by Mr. Beasley, Echo, Brandon, and half the camp. They're all staring up at me, waiting for me to make my descent. They do not look like, pardon the expression, happy campers.

When I'm safely on the ground, Mr. Beasley shuffles over and makes a snooty but annoyed face at me.

"Give me one good reason why you shouldn't be dismissed from my camp!"

"Good reason one, Swiss Miss," says Echo.

"W-w-well," I start, but Brandon cuts me off.

"Because Jacky Hart is an inspiration to us all!" he says, pushing his way to the front of the crowd. "She is completely and totally dedicated to her craft! You want to talk about total immersion, Mr. Beasley? Jacky Hart walks that talk!"

"Oh, really?" Mr. Beasley and Echo say simultaneously.

"Ha!" scoffs Ashley, who has joined the crowd. (I think she needed time to do her hair and makeup before making her dramatic entrance.)

"Scoff if you will, Ashley," says Brandon.

"Oh, I'm scoffing all right...."

"But Miss Hart is going to be the egg in my show *Scrambled Egg*. To do so convincingly, she needs to know how it feels to be stranded high above a skillet, staring down at her destiny—the frying pan. And so, like all our most dedicated actors—Olivier, Brando, Streep, Caroline Jean Risvold—she must first create a sensory memory of that feeling." He points up to the tree limb where I recently roosted. "Mr. Beasley, fellow artistes, Jacky's actions this evening do not call for dismissal. No. They call for praise, honor, and accolades. For there will be no pretending in my piece. There will be only truth and honest emotions! Come Saturday night, Jacqueline Hart will BE the egg!"

"Marvelous!" shouts Madame Lamond with a gasp. I guess she likes artsy stuff even when it isn't dance.

"Give the girl a badge, Mr. Beasley!" cries the acting teacher who had us do that shriveling-bacon improv in class.

"Kick her out!" shouts Ashley. "Jacky's wacky!"

Echo leans in and whispers something into Mr. Beasley's ear.

He doesn't look happy to hear it.

"Fine," he finally says. "Well said, Brandon." He turns to me and strokes his beard. "I'm so looking forward to your performance this weekend, Miss Hart."

"So forward looking, Miss Hart, weak knees," says Echo.

"I'm sure your 'sponsor' will be pleased."

"Sponsor pleased."

Then, as my heart sinks, Mr. Beasley turns to the crowd of campers.

"Oh, didn't you all know?" he says with a smirk.

"Didn't you know, oh?" Echo is smirking, too.

"Know what?" demands Ashley, placing both her hands on her hips and giving the world her most petulant pout.

Mr. Beasley sneers. "Miss Hart is only here at Camp Footlights because Latoya Sherron is footing the bill. Jacky Hart is a charity case."

"Charity case" is all Echo repeats.

"Oh, my," says Ashley coyly.

Yep. I've been outed. Everybody knows my secret.

I'm nothing but a poor kid from New Jersey who doesn't belong in the same camp or the same league as all these rich superstars.

CHAPTER 27

Oh, your poor, poor parents," Ashley sighs at me on Saturday afternoon. "First, they're literally poor, otherwise—hello—you wouldn't be a charity case. Second, they're driving all the way up from *New Jersey* to see you play a fried egg."

When she says "New Jersey," it sounds like she's talking about a contagious tropical disease—the kind that would give you a rash.

"Too bad you didn't take my dance rehearsal more seriously," she continues. "Just think—you could've been onstage with me! Instead of being a goofball washout, you could've told your children about how, once upon a time, you were onstage with the one and only Ashley Jones! Sad. So sad."

She struts away and Brooklyn comes over to buck me up.

"Don't let Ashley get under your dome, Jacky," she says. "She's just a major buzzkill."

We're in the barn theater. Every show in the Saturday night showcase was given a time slot for its technical rehearsal. That means we're running through the sound and light cues and rehearsing in our costumes.

Yes, that also means I look like a fried egg and Brooklyn looks like a dog. I mean, she's in a dog costume. Not that she's unattractive. In fact, Brooklyn is super-pretty. She's in that Latoya Sherron glam girl league.

Ashley with an Exclamation Point gets the first tech rehearsal, even though it will be the last performance in the showcase because, as Mr. Beasley puts it, "We always save the best for last."

Guess who'll be up first? You guessed it. Me and the two strips of bacon. And, in the middle of our tech run-through (we had the last spot for that), one of the bacon bits quits.

"I just don't feel the sputter," she tells Brandon.

So, yep, the playwright has to slip into the role

with no rehearsal. Fortunately, he knows all the lines. He should. He wrote 'em.

I have to climb a twelve-foot ladder and jump onto a dark gray trampoline. It's our cast-iron skillet. I'm kind of happy that I had that trial run up the tree with the raccoon. Twelve feet up a ladder is nothing compared with that.

My whole family is set to arrive at Camp Footlights around seven thirty. Curtain is at eight, so I can't say hi until after the show. Seven thirty is our half-hour call. That means we have to be in the dressing room, not out front greeting our fans and family, which in my case are one and the same.

I cheat a little and look out one of the dressing room windows. They're high, narrow, and tilted open to let in a cool summer breeze. I have to climb up on a chair to reach one.

Peering out into the parking lot, I can see Mom, Dad, and all my sisters.

Another car pulls in right beside theirs. It's Ms. O'Mara with some of the Seaside Heights theater kids—Bill, Jeff, and Dan.

I tap on the glass and wave.

"Hey, you guys!"

I'm about to whistle when Queen Ashley speaks from her place at the makeup table.

"Greeting the audience before the show is sooooo unprofessional," she advises everybody within ten yards of her makeup mirror.

I hop off that chair so fast, I almost twist my ankle. That is not what they mean when, for good luck, they tell you to break a leg before a show. That saying has something to do with bending your knee when you take a bow. Or ancient Greek audiences stomping their feet instead of clapping their hands. There might've been an orthopedic surgeon involved in coming up with the expression, too. No one really knows.

By the way, Ashley's place at the makeup table is twice as wide as anybody else's, and she has three times the number of lightbulbs framing her mirror.

"That's where Caroline Jean Risvold used to put on her makeup," Michael tells me as he helps zip up the back of my egg suit. "The star of the summer always gets that spot."

So at least I know where in the barn theater dressing room I'll *never* be sitting.

Brandon comes in, wearing his bacon costume.

Stephanie Douglas is with him. They both look delicious.

Brandon hands Stephanie a small squirt bottle.

"Spritz some of this under your arms and behind your ears," says Brandon.

"Why?" asks Stephanie.

"So you'll smell like bacon. This is immersive theater. We're going for total sensory overload."

Fortunately, Brandon doesn't have any spray that'll make me smell like an egg. Fried, rotten, or otherwise.

But let me just say, waiting backstage with Brandon and Stephanie to open the Saturday showcase, remembering that I skipped dinner because I was nervous, and breathing in the delicious scent of bacon?

Your mother got hungry, girls. Super-hungry.

CHAPTER 28

I'm happy to report that I get some pretty big laughs.

Sure, Brandon gave me all sorts of punny lines. (He may be a genius, but come on, he's ten!)

I tell the audience that being an egg "isn't all that it's cracked up to be." When it's time to climb the ladder, I say, "I'll scramble up it."

I mug a funny-enough face to cover the corn popping out of my mouth, and people forget what I just said.

I do pick up a few more laughs at the top of the ladder when I look into the dusty spotlight beam and ask the heavens above, "Oh, why, oh, why do hens lay eggs?" When no answer comes, I shake my fist and shout my own answer into the dark void. "Because if they dropped 'em, they'd break."

I sell it hard and earn a huge guffaw.

Then the bacon strips call up to me.

"Do you think this outfit is too hammy?" asks Brandon, turning around so I can examine the marbled backside of his bacon costume.

"Jump in!" he and Stephanie shout. They also make snap, sizzle, and pop sounds. They're the porkier version of Rice Krispies.

"Have no fear," says Brandon, giving me my cue. "We've both been cured!"

Then, yes, I do my pratfall.

I jump off the ladder, land on my butt, and bounce around on the trampoline.

"Hey, that tub of yogurt over there just insulted me!" says Brandon when I settle in next to him.

"Really?" I ask. "What'd the yogurt say?"

"It called me an uncultured swine!"

"So how do we end this bit?" says Stephanie. That's what Brandon calls breaking the fourth wall. As part of our theater piece, we let the audience know *we* know it's a theater piece.

I actually get to wink at the crowd. "Easy," I say.

"It's over. And so am I." I flip onto my belly. "I'm over easy!"

The lights dim. The crowd applauds. Kind of.

I think Brandon's work might be a little too avant-garde for this audience of friends and families. (*Avant-garde* means it's new, unconventional, and kind of weird.)

On the other hand, they all seem to love *Ashley with an Exclamation Point*! We had eggs and bacon. Ashley has the razzle-dazzle of song and dance.

At the final curtain call, when all the kids in the showcase come onstage to take one big bow together, Ashley stands in the center of the line. She doesn't hold hands with the performers on either side of her like the rest of us do. Ashley's hands are busy. Picking up all the bouquets of roses that people (including Mr. Beasley) are tossing at her feet.

CHAPTER 29

loved it," Ms. O'Mara tells me after the show. "It's good to see you having so much fun up there! Just keep being yourself, Jacky."

"No," says my big sister Sophia. "Pick someone better."

We're all in the parking lot, saying our goodbyes.

"I thought it was egg-cellent," says Jeff Cohen. Yeah. He and Brandon are a lot alike.

Dan says I was "egg-ceptionally good."

Leaving Bill to say I made a great "egg-zit."

I cock an eyebrow. "Is that a pimple joke, Bill?"

He looks shocked. Like I caught him saying something bad. "No," he says. "I was, you know, playing off the word *exit*."

"Oh," I say, pretending that I'm just now getting it. "Well, when you egg-splain it like that..."

Bill smiles. He finally realizes I'm just messing with him.

My Shakespeare Down the Shore friends climb into Ms. O'Mara's car and take off. It's time to face my family.

"Good show," says Mom. "These kids up here are all so talented."

"I liked the dancing dogs!" says Emma. She's six. Of course she likes dancing dogs more than bouncing eggs.

"That Ashley is amazing," gushes super-sweet Hannah. "She can sing, dance, and act! I bet she even makes her own costumes."

Uh, no, I want to say. *That's all Michael.*

But Riley talks first. "I can see why they called it *Ashley with an Exclamation Point*! It was fantastic, with an exclamation point."

Sophia has eyes for Michael, who passes by toting a laundry basket. "What's *his* name? He reminds me of bacon because he's sizzlin' hot."

"That's Michael," I tell her. "He designed all the costumes in all the shows."

"Huh," says Sophia. "I guess everybody who looks good can't sing and perform like that Ashley Jones. Sadly, some seriously good-looking people just end up doing other people's laundry."

"Your friend Brooklyn can really dance," says Victoria with a great air of authority because, don't forget, she knows everything about everything. "In her dog costume, she reminded me of that time you played Snoopy. Now that was a good part. In a good show."

The way she says it? It's clear she thinks my egg was a bad part in a bad show.

"Brooklyn's my roommate," I tell her.

"Perfect. Then you can pass on a little advice. She needs a last name. All the famous dancers have them. Paula Abdul. Ginger Rogers. Martha Graham."

"What about Madonna?"

Victoria crinkles her nose and shakes her head. "She's more of a singer. If you call what she does singing..."

It's nearly ten thirty at night, and my family has a long drive home to the Jersey Shore. We say our goodbyes.

Dad gives me a hug.

"I'm so glad you were able to come to this camp this summer," he says.

That makes me smile.

"At least you'll get this showbiz bug out of your system. When school starts in the fall, you can really focus on hitting the books."

So, yeah.

My first big showcase performance at Camp Footlights? If I'd listened to my family, it would've definitely been my last.

CHAPTER 30

he next night, Sunday, there's a Footsie Awards
ceremony at Camp Footlights.

Really? I think. *This session has only been going
for a week and they're already handing out awards?*

"They do it every week after the Saturday showcase," Brooklyn explains.

"And next Saturday," says Michael, "there won't
be a showcase. Everybody will be in the same show:
The Footlights Revue. We do it every summer."

"When are the auditions?" I ask.

"Tomorrow afternoon," says Brandon.

"Oh, by the way," Michael says to me, "if you win
an award tonight and want to keep your trophy, you
have to pay for it. The ones they hand out here at the

ceremony are symbolic only. Also, if you want a copy of the official photo they snap of you holding your symbolic trophy, that costs extra, too."

"This whole Footsie Awards deal is what they call a cash cow for Camp Footlights," adds Brandon. "You ever wonder how they came up with that expression? I mean, if your cow starts squirting out cash instead of milk, it might be time to move your dairy farm a little farther away from the nuclear power plant."

The four of us are sitting at a table in the cavernous dining hall, where the award ceremony takes place. Mr. Beasley is the master of ceremonies, and, yes, Echo repeats everything he says to the unlucky kids seated at her table.

There isn't much suspense in any of the categories. You guessed it. Ashley Jones graciously accepts the Footsies for Best Singer, Best Performer, and Best Choreography. She shares that last one with Madame Lamond but only because Madame Lamond is a dancer and, therefore, extremely spry. She beats Ashley in the sprint to the podium. Ashley also goes home with the Broadway-Bound and Superstar of the Summer trophies.

I wonder about that last one. The summer session

isn't over for two more weeks. Guess Mr. Beasley just wants to cut to the chase.

Brooklyn picks up a Footsie for Best Supporting Dancer, and Michael scores one for Best Use of Sequins for Making a Star Shimmer for his work on *Ashley with an Exclamation Point*!

At the end of the very long and seriously boring ceremony (there's no band to play Ashley off when she gives her fifth acceptance speech), Brandon and I, along with two dozen other campers, are awarded

Good Sport trophies. They're basically given to everybody who didn't win anything else.

Yes, girls, that was my very first theatrical award. Fortunately, it wouldn't be my last.

Also fortunately, all of us Good Sports didn't have to make an acceptance speech.

If we did, I think I would've said, *Thank you. I'm mortified.*

And, no, I did not ask Latoya Sherron to pay an extra $9.99 so I could take my plastic trophy home.

CHAPTER 31

Believe it or not, my second week at camp starts with something fun!

Brooklyn and I sign up for an Acting in Commercials class. It's taught by Chuck Binkley. A real advertising executive from New York City. The class is held in one of the camp's rehearsal rooms.

"Think of a thirty-second spot as a very short short film," Mr. Binkley tells us. "It's a chance to show millions of people what you've got. You know Brad Pitt, the handsome dude who did that guest shot on *21 Jump Street*? He got his start doing a Pringles commercial in 1988. That other guy, Keanu Reeves, the one who starred in *Bill and Ted's*

Excellent Adventure? One of his first jobs was a Coke commercial back in eighty-three! Commercials are a great way to polish your acting chops and make a little money while you go to auditions for Broadway shows, movies, and TV pilots."

I like commercials. A lot of them are funny. Some have fun jingles, like that "I don't want to grow up, I'm a Toys 'R' Us kid." I always sing along with that one whenever it comes on TV.

(BTW, Grace and Tina—Toys "R" Us was a big, humongous toy superstore back in the days when people shopped in big, humongous superstores instead of on the Internet.)

"Acting in commercials," Mr. Binkley tells us, "is all about saying the most with the least number of words. Think of them as haiku poems. Compact and concise."

He passes out a script for what he calls "voice-over copy."

"That means an off-camera announcer reads it over the action of the scene. Trust me, kids—there're big bucks in voice-overs. If you're the voice-over performer, you get paid every single time the commercial airs. And all you have to do is spend an hour or so in a recording studio reading a line or two of copy."

There are only eight words on the script Mr. Binkley passes around the room: "Maxwell House coffee. Good to the last drop."

Brandon, who's in the class with us, raises his hand.

"Yeah?" says Mr. Binkley. "Question?"

"Yes, sir. I've always wondered about this slogan. If Maxwell House coffee is good to the last drop, what's wrong with that last drop? How'd it go bad? What did all the other drops have that it didn't?"

"Good question. I'll ask Mr. Maxwell the next time I'm at his house. But, for now, let's focus on giving the line a good reading, okay?"

"Cool," says Brandon. "I'm down with that."

Mr. Binkley nods at me. "Why don't you go first," he says.

"Um, okay."

He motions for me to come to the front of the room.

"What's your name?" he asks.

"Jacky. Jacky Hart."

"Oh, Jacky Hart. Sell me a can of coffee beans."

I study the script. I screw on my serious face. I'm ready to sell some beans!

"Maxwell House coffee," I say super-smoothly. "Good to the last drop."

Mr. Binkley shakes his head. "You're not selling how good it is."

So I try again. "Maxwell House coffee. GOOD to the last drop."

Another head shake. "How long is it good?"

"Um, until the last drop."

"Okay. Let me hear it."

I try again. "Maxwell House coffee. GOOD to the LAST drop."

"Can you give it more of a smile? But don't forget. The product name is the most important part of any commercial."

I smile until my cheeks hurt. "MAXWELL HOUSE coffee." I practically scream the brand name. "GOOD to the LAST DROP!"

Mr. Binkley bobbles his head back and forth. He is not pleased. "Try not to be so selly. You're pushing way too hard."

This goes on for about ten minutes.

For my final read, I'm whispering with friendly but knowing authority and, for some reason, emphasizing "House" and "drop."

"Maxwell **HOUSE** coffee. Good to the last **DROP**!"

"O-kay," says Mr. Binkley. "Good work. Let's leave it there."

I think my line readings are boring him.

"Sorry to be so late," says Ashley, sweeping into the room. "I had to do a radio interview about winning all those awards yesterday." She thrusts out her hand. "Where's my ad copy?"

"And you are?" says Mr. Binkley.

Ashley chuckles. She expects everybody who sets foot on the Camp Footlights campus to know who she is. She also expects them to want her autograph. "I'm Ashley Jones, the actress who was born to read your script, no matter what it says."

Mr. Binkley nods. He's impressed. "I like your attitude, Ashley. You've got IT, kid."

"I just hope *it* isn't contagious," mumbles Brandon.

Ashley gives the teacher her *Gimme-gimme* gesture. He hands her the script.

She glances at it. For maybe two seconds. Then she says, "Maxwell House coffee. Good...to the last drop."

"Booyah!" says Mr. Binkley. "Nailed it!"

Ashley blinks and beams. Brooklyn and I roll our eyes. Especially when Mr. Binkley tells Ashley he knows a commercial agent who's looking for "fresh faces with mad talent."

Why do I think that Ashley Jones will be starring in Pringles and Coke commercials of her own before the summer's done?

CHAPTER 32

We have a two-hour break after our Acting in Commercials class.

Well, those of us who aren't Ashley have a break. She has to call the commercial talent agent Mr. Binkley mentioned "right away!"

"Hey," says Brandon when we're all just hanging out after class, "we should do a parody commercial. Like they do on *Saturday Night Live*! We should do one for Maxwell *Mouse* coffee!"

"It's good to the last drop," I say, "because it's brewed from mouse droppings."

Brooklyn scrunches up her face. "Gross and disgusting, Jacky."

"What?" I reply with mock shock. "Mouse droppings are brown, so is coffee!"

Brooklyn cracks up.

"Hang here, you two," she says. "I have a camcorder up in the room. You guys write the script, then we can shoot it."

"Who gets to play the mouse?" I ask.

"Ashley!" shouts Brooklyn as she dashes back to the lodge to grab her video gear. "She plays all the parts in everything!"

Brandon and I crack each other up, bouncing lines around, writing a thirty-second commercial about a mouse who makes the world's most disgusting cup of coffee.

"The best part of waking up," I say, "is something slimy in your cup."

Brandon starts crooning a jingle based on the Chock Full o' Nuts commercials. *"Chock Full o' Mouse is that heavenly coffee, heavenly coffee. Better coffee Mickey Mouse's money can't buy!"*

By the time Brooklyn is back with the camera, we've moved on to a whole new idea.

Brooklyn will fake-drink a cup of coffee and start dancing, faster and faster.

We give Maxwell House a new slogan (because Brandon is still wondering what went wrong with that last drop to make it no good). After she does her jittery jitterbug (which, by the way, is hysterical), Brooklyn looks down the barrel of the camera lens and says, "Maxwell House. We put the perk in your percolator."

Because, kids, a percolator—an electric coffeepot that bubbles water through coffee grounds—is what people used to use to make coffee before there was a Starbucks to make it for them. Yes, this all took place in a time when America did not yet run on Dunkin'.

Anyway, we think our coffee commercial parody is hilarious.

But there's only one way to be sure. We need an audience.

"Let's show it to Michael!" I say.

"Great idea," say Brooklyn and Brandon.

So we all tear across the open field, heading for the barn theater and the downstairs costume shop. Brooklyn has the video camera. The tape inside has our commercial spoof. Michael will be able to watch it on the swing-out viewfinder.

We yank open the STAFF ONLY door and trundle down the staircase to the basement.

I'm leading the way.

But I freeze when I hit the bottom step.

Because I hear something. It's wafting up the hall from the costume shop.

It's this amazing Irish tenor voice singing a show tune.

"She's just a girl, an ev'ryday girl."

"That's 'I Met a Girl,'" whispers Brooklyn while the voice keeps singing. "From the 1960 MGM movie musical *Bells Are Ringing*."

"Music by Jule Styne," says ten-year-old Brandon. "Lyrics by Betty Comden and Adolph Green."

I'm impressed that they both know so much about classic show tunes.

But I'm even more impressed by the guy singing the song.

Michael, the costume shop kid, has an incredible voice! And I can't help but wonder if he's singing about me!

Hey, I'm a girl. We just met.

It's a possibility.

CHAPTER 33

We just hang at the door for a few minutes and soak up the magnificence of Michael's voice.

He moves on to "Some Enchanted Evening" from the Broadway classic *South Pacific*. It's all about how, on some enchanted evening, "you may see a stranger across a crowded room."

And once again, I wonder if Michael is singing about me.

Sure, we first saw each other in the afternoon, not the evening, and it wasn't very enchanted. In fact, it was kind of a bummer for me, since I'd just been kicked out of Ashley's show. And the room where we met wasn't very crowded. Just me, Michael, Brooklyn, and a bunch of mannequins.

But still. We were strangers when we met. He *could* be singing about me. In code.

But what's more important is how fantastically he sings! Of course he played the lead in *Oliver!* six years ago. He is an amazingly talented tenor. So, I have to wonder, *Why is he down here in the costume shop when he should be upstairs at center stage, still singing in the spotlight?*

He hits the big finish: *"Once you have found her, never...let...her...GO!!!"*

Michael hasn't yet seen us gawking at his back from the doorway. But when he finishes, we burst into applause and start cheering.

"Bravo!" shouts Brandon. "Bravo!"

Brooklyn and I are giving Michael a chorus of *woo-hoo*s!

He whips around from his sewing machine. His face blushes a bright pink (and not from too much sun).

"Um, how long have you guys been lurking there?" he asks.

"Long enough to know you should be back upstairs on the main stage starring in every single show!" I say.

"Except, of course, *Ashley with an Exclamation Point*," cracks Brandon. "Then again, that show should just be outlawed entirely. Or at least come with a warning about how it may cause nausea."

"You have an incredible singing voice, Michael," adds Brooklyn. "Absolutely incredible."

"Thanks," says Michael, dropping his eyes. "I used to think so, too."

"You *used* to?" I say. "Hello—did you not just hear yourself?"

"Yeah. I hear me all the time. Singing is just something I do for fun, now. Sure, when I first came to Camp Footlights, I thought I had talent. I guess every kid who comes here thinks that. In fact, back in the day, Ashley and I starred in a lot of the junior stage shows. We were both ten years old our first summer. She was way more fun before she went to middle school. Then, three summers ago, she refused to 'be seen onstage' with me. So I drifted down here. Discovered another talent. Costume design."

"Can't you do both?" I ask. "Sing in shows and do costume design?"

"I thought about it. In fact, this was the summer I was going to start auditioning again. But then Mr. Beasley was appointed the new director of Camp Footlights. And his first official act? Crowning Ashley 'Queen of Everything.'"

Michael takes a deep breath and tells us he's glad he "learned early" that he wasn't "cut out" for the "cutthroat world" of show business.

"Ashley and Mr. Beasley are both right," he adds. "I'm better off down here."

I feel so sorry for Michael. Some very bad people (I'm looking at you, Ashley Jones and Mr. Beasley) took his dream and crushed it.

We forget all about our goofy commercial parody.

We just sit and listen to Michael's sad story. Yes, girls, at that instant, your mother was seriously crushing on Michael, the costume shop kid, even though I didn't know his last name. (And, yes, I told your father, the young Bill Phillips, all about Michael when I was back home in Seaside Heights. Of course, I didn't tell him until, oh, five years later, but I told him.)

"Six years ago, Ashley and I were best friends," Michael says. "And then, three years later, poof! We weren't." He sighs. "It went from bad to horrible. This summer, Mr. Beasley made it even worse. He's like a helium tank constantly inflating her ego balloon." He gives us a shrug. "People change. Relationships change. Dreams can change, too."

"So is this really your dream?" I ask, opening my arms to take in the costume shop.

"It's fun. I'm good at it. People, for the most part, leave me alone."

"But is it your *dream*, Michael?" asks Brooklyn.

"Yes," says Michael. "Sort of. Okay, it's my fall-back dream. I think everybody should have one. Just in case your first dream really doesn't want you dreaming it anymore."

He turns back to his sewing machine and presses the foot pedal. The needle starts pumping up and down as he feeds fabric through it.

"Sorry," he says. "I can't really hang. I have to alter a ton of costumes this week. The all-camp musical is Saturday. Yes, *The Footlights Revue* is the exact same show every summer, but the performers change. The costumes have to change with them."

"You should be in the show," I tell Michael.

"Excuse me?" he says.

"You said it's a musical."

He nods. "It's a collection of show tunes."

"Which you were just singing."

"It's true," says Brandon. "We all heard you doing it."

"You need to go to the auditions this afternoon," insists Brooklyn.

Michael laughs. "Ha! I stopped doing the revue three summers ago. I don't think 'Some Enchanted Evening' is even in the rundown."

"Well," I say, "we think it's time you started doing the show again. It's time you showed Mr. Beasley and Ashley and everybody who you really are, Michael. You may think your first-choice dream doesn't want you dreaming it, but we disagree. Because our dream is hearing you sing like that at center stage!"

"Exactly," says Brandon. "You doing it instead of Ashley."

We all give him a side-eye look.

"What? Did I go too far?" Brandon says. "I do that sometimes. It's my superpower."

CHAPTER 34

That afternoon, we're all upstairs in the barn theater, ready to audition for *The Footlights Revue.* Yes, Michael is there with us.

Which is why we are sitting in the last row. In the dark.

"I don't want Mr. Beasley to see me," he whispers. "I'm supposed to be downstairs making hats for the *Yankee Doodle Dandy* number."

"I wrote my own audition song," says Brandon. "Well, my own lyrics. The tune I borrowed from *Ashley with an Exclamation Point.* That 'My Best Friend Is Me' number." He starts singing. Badly. I think Brandon is tone-deaf.

"Sorry, Mr. Beasley, can't you see
This is how it's gotta be?
We know you may disagree,
But we can't stand Ash-lee!
No, we can't stand Ash-LEEEEE!"

"Um, you might want to sing something else," I suggest.

"Yeah," says Brooklyn. "That didn't sound like it was written in your key."

"I know some songs you could talk-sing," says Michael, very kindly. "That's what Rex Harrison did in *My Fair Lady*."

"Nah," says Brandon. "I'm just goofing around. I'm not going to sing at all. I'm not even going to audition. I don't have to. The camp counselors have already assigned me my role for the show."

"Oh, really?" I say. "Who are you going to be?"

"The head usher," says Brandon. "It's an audience favorite every year because the head usher hands out the programs and shows people where to sit. Besides, as you three just so painfully witnessed, it should probably be illegal for me to sing in public."

At three o'clock on the dot, Mr. Beasley and Echo march onstage.

"Welcome, everybody, to the annual auditions for *The Footlights Revue*, our all-camp musical!"

"Musical camp annual auditions," says Echo.

Everyone applauds. We clap along, too.

"As is customary," Mr. Beasley continues, "we will open the show with a rousing rendition of 'There's No Business Like Show Business' from *Annie Get Your Gun*."

(I can't wait to hear how Echo mangles that mouthful.)

"Annie like your rousing show business no business get a gun." She does not disappoint.

Counselors walk through the auditorium passing out sheet music for "There's No Business Like Show Business." I go ahead and take one, even though I'm really only there to support Michael.

"Ashley?" says Mr. Beasley. "Why don't you come up here and show everybody how it's done."

"Show done," echoes Echo.

Ashley bounds onstage. The piano accompanist awaits his cue.

Ashley basks in the glow of the stage lights for a moment or so. Then she gives the pianist the slightest nod.

He starts plinking keys. She starts belting out notes. Ashley's voice rings off the rafters. She's louder than the lady from the original cast album I heard sing the song on Mom and Dad's record player, and that lady was LOUD.

Ashley does only sixteen bars of the song, a standard length for an audition, but she is almost as good as she is loud.

She turns to Mr. Beasley. "Do you still want anybody else to audition?" she asks.

He chuckles. Echo chuckles.

"Yes, Ashley. The whole camp will be involved in the show, as is the tradition."

"*Tra-di-tion*," says Echo, doing it like that song from *Fiddler on the Roof.*

"You can't sing every single song in the show," Mr. Beasley continues. "It's two hours long. You'd wear yourself out."

Ashley huffs and puffs a little then, accepting the cold hard truth, exits stage right, and heads to her seat in the front row.

190

"Now then," says Mr. Beasley, "to streamline things…"

"Line the stream with things," says Echo.

"…because time is precious and I'm due over at the Beef 'n' Boards Dinner Theater, where I am, of course, the artistic director, the camp staff and I have made some preliminary decisions. Brandon Maloney will be our head usher. Brooklyn will be the lead dancer for 'All That Jazz.'"

"Jazz hands," says Echo, splaying out the fingers on both her hands and shaking them enthusiastically.

We give Brooklyn's star turn in the chorus line a hearty "Booyah!" cheer. She gives us her "jazz hands" in return.

Mr. Beasley goes down a list of about a dozen other names and assignments, ably echoed by Echo. Finally, he gets to me.

"Jacky Hart?" He peers out into the audience.

I raise my hand.

"You've only been here a week, so you'll be on the *Footlights Revue* tech crew. Follow spot operator. It'll be a great way for you to learn what it takes to star in a *real* show."

Ashley stands up at her seat in the front row.

"Because, for most of the show, you and your spot-light will be following me!"

"Okay," says Mr. Beasley, "we do have a few other singing roles."

"Bread and butter rolls," says Echo. (Maybe she's thinking about Mr. Beasley's other gig at that dinner theater.)

Mr. Beasley smiles at the audience, which he can't actually see because stage lights are blinding him. "Who would like to come up and audition next?"

Brandon, Brooklyn, and I swivel to face Michael.

"Go on," we whisper. "Go for it."

Michael raises his hand and stands up.

"Uh, I'll go next."

Mr. Beasley shields his eyes with his hand. "Michael?"

"Yes, sir." He's ready to bound up the center aisle and take the stage.

But Mr. Beasley holds up his hand like a traffic cop to stop him.

Michael stops.

Mr. Beasley shakes his head. "Michael, Michael, Michael," he sighs.

"Michael," sighs Echo. "Michael, Michael."

"We've discussed this," says Mr. Beasley. "You're not a singer. You sew stitches."

"See Michael sew stitches by the seashore," says Echo.

"You're supposed to be making *Yankee Doodle* hats, aren't you?" says Mr. Beasley.

"Doodle poodle Yankee yoodle" comes the echo.

Michael nods. He understands. He turns around and exits the auditorium.

He never gets to take his shot.

Because, sometimes, there really is no business like show business.

Other businesses are much more fair.

CHAPTER 35

That night in our dorm room, Brooklyn and I are still steaming about what Mr. Beasley did to Michael.

"I think Camp Footlights was better back in the day," says Brooklyn. "Like last summer. Before, somehow, someway, Mr. Beasley got the top job."

"Where'd they find him?" I fume.

Brooklyn shrugs. "Maybe at that Beef 'n' Boards Dinner Theater where, as he constantly reminds everybody, he's the artistic director."

"What?" I say. "Does he choreograph the prime rib and baked potatoes? Does he make sure the dessert Jell-O jiggles in time to the music?"

I hear the phone ring out in the hall. Yes, in 1991,

none of us had our own personal phones and data plans. We had pay phones hanging on walls. None of those phones had any apps, either. Just a slot where you needed to drop a quarter if you wanted to hear a dial tone, something else phones don't really have anymore.

Someone knocks on our door. It's Annalyse Lily Hatfield from down the hall.

"The phone's for you, Jacky," she says.

"Thanks, Annalyse," I say.

I hurry into the hall, wondering if everything is okay at home.

"Hello?" I say, closing my eyes because I'm afraid a ten o'clock call to Camp Footlights can only mean bad news.

"Hey, Jacky."

I breathe a sigh of relief. It's my oldest sister, Sydney. She didn't come see my brilliant performance as a diving egg with the rest of the family because she's taking summer school classes. At Princeton University. She's a scholarship student, too. The brainy kind.

"Hiya, Sydney!"

"Sorry for the late call."

"That's okay."

"I just wanted to check in with you, Jacky. Mom and Dad told me about that show you did. *Scrambled Egg*. Sounds wacky."

I nod. "It was."

"So," says Sydney, "how are things up at camp?"

And—BOOM. I'm off. That's all the setup and intro I need.

"Things are pretty messed up, Sydney," I tell her. "There's this great kid, a guy named Michael, and he can really sing. Like an angel. Not that I've ever heard an angel sing. Most of the angels I've met are statues or the imaginary one on my shoulder, but you have to figure the real ones sing great, especially Harold. You know. The guy from that Christmas carol. 'Hark, Harold the Angel Sings.'"

Brooklyn steps out of our room to give me a quizzical look.

"But they won't let Michael sing. And there's an angel named Michael, although usually, I think he plays the trumpet."

Now Brooklyn is shaking her head and laughing.

Annalyse Lily Hatfield comes out of her room. So do a couple of other girls. But not Ashley. She's not in our dorm. As the star of the summer, she has a small, private cabin. (I'm starting to wonder if Ashley's parents made a sizable contribution to Camp Footlights or something to make sure their daughter got the royal treatment.)

"There's one girl up here who thinks she's all that and a bag of chips," I say, because, yes, that was an expression we used for someone who was too big for their britches, because none of us knew what britches were. "She gets all the leads in all the shows. And the camp director? Oh, he's her biggest fan. Echo is right there with him, though. That's not her real name, it's just what everybody calls her because she echoes whatever her boss says, which is usually something gushy about that girl I just told you about. Her name is Ashley. With an exclamation point. Ashley didn't want me being a dancing dog, so I did that wacky show where I was an egg, which actually was kind of fun. Of course, this was after I climbed a tree and got spooked by a raccoon. Fortunately, my new friends rescued me. Well, actually, the volunteer fire department rescued me, but they wouldn't've known that I was up a tree if Brooklyn hadn't found me. Not the whole borough. My friend Brooklyn. She's from Brooklyn. And, man, can she dance."

I look up the hall.

Everybody is out of their rooms.

They're all smiling at me.

"So basically, sis, I think we're all tired of Ashley hogging the spotlight when everybody at this camp is super-talented or they wouldn't be here."

"Yeah!" says Annalyse and a few other members of my impromptu audience.

"I mean, I'm only here because Latoya Sherron thinks I'm talented. We can talk about that because, thanks to Mr. Beasley, everybody already knows I'm a charity case."

"No," shouts Brooklyn. "You're a scholarship student!"

"Yeah!" agrees my audience. "You're a scholarship student!"

Whoa. For a second, I feel like Mr. Beasley. I have my own echo.

"So, Sydney," I say, wrapping up my answer, "in short, camp is tough. But I'm reminded of the guy who had a job shoveling elephant poop at the circus. One night, he was complaining to his buddies about his work. 'My arms are tired. My shoes and my pants are a mess. I stink all the time.' His friends all said, 'So why don't you quit and find another job?' The guy looked at them, stunned. 'What?' he said. 'And give up show business?'"

My hallway audience applauds.

Sydney laughs. "Good," she says. "You're still you, Jacky. That's what I needed to hear."

We say our goodbyes. I hang up. And I realize that's what I needed to hear, too.

I'm still me.

And maybe it's time to be even more me!

CHAPTER 36

Unfortunately, the next day, nobody really wants to see or hear much of me being me.

I'm up on a catwalk that hangs over the auditorium seats. I'm in a metal box, being introduced to my follow spot. Mr. Leonard Skaggs, the camp's tech director and the *Footlights Revue* stage manager, gives me a quick how-to lesson.

"This here is your Super Trouper," he says. "It utilizes a high-intensity carbon arc lamp, which will produce a snow-white circle of light that'll set your spotlighted performer apart from all the other schlubs onstage with 'em. You can swing it left, swing it right. Tilt it up and down. Your douser here controls the intensity of your beam. The iris there controls the beam size. You can make it wider, like so, or tighter, like so. Any questions?"

Yes, I want to say. *Is this the absolute worst job you can give someone who dreams of being* in *the spotlight themselves?*

But I don't. I just say, "No, sir. I think I've got it."

After all, I'm a reliable and uncomplaining person. A true trouper. And now I'm a trouper operating a Super Trouper.

Mr. Skaggs gives me a headset.

"I'll give you your cues over this," he says. "But we keep it simple. Wherever Ashley Jones goes, you follow her."

And that's what I do.

For three hours.

I swing my spotlight left; I swing it right. I keep Ashley bathed in her bright circle of white. I widen it. I tighten it.

I wish my spotlight were the locomotive beacon of an oncoming train and Ashley was tied to my train tracks.

I wish I could shine my spotlight on Brooklyn, dancing in the background. Even her big number, "All That Jazz," is sung by Ashley. So guess who gets to bathe in the bright circle? The singer, not the dancer.

The only thing I hear on my headset is Mr. Skaggs coaching me to "Stay with Ashley. Stay with Ashley."

Finally, Mr. Beasley wraps rehearsal for the day.

"Everybody? Back here tomorrow at three. I want you off book. I want your choreography memorized. And Leonard?"

"Yes?" comes Mr. Skaggs's voice from his stage manager desk off in the wings.

"Work with your follow spot operator. The transitions were a little herky-jerky today! I want them as smooth as silk!"

Great. The head of Camp Footlights doesn't even like the way I shove a light beam around his stage.

CHAPTER 37

After rehearsal, Brooklyn, Brandon, and I head downstairs to the costume shop to see if Michael needs any help.

Brandon had even less to do at the rehearsal than me. As head usher in an empty auditorium, he didn't have anybody to "ush."

"So how'd it go?" asks Michael, running more sequined material through his sewing machine.

"Absolutely fantastic," says Brandon. "But only if your name is Ashley Jones."

"Is she doing all the big numbers?" Michael asks.

"Yep," says Brooklyn. "Even the one from *Phantom of the Opera*. She's playing the Phantom."

"I used to sing that song," Michael mutters.

"Well, they gave it to Ashley this year," I say. "But you can't really tell it's her. The mask covers half her face."

"It's a start," says Brandon. (He'd probably be called "snarky" by kids today.)

I see a glitter-spangled cowboy hat sitting on a worktable. I pop it onto my head and put on a Southern twang. "Well, kiss my grits, y'all. I'm the Phantom of the Grand Ole Opry. I'm as country as a baked bean sandwich."

Brooklyn grabs a feathered boa, wraps it around her neck, and fans herself. "Excuse me. I'm Ashley Jones. Perhaps you've heard of me?"

"Well, of course I heard a' you," I tell her, miming like I need to spit out a plunk of chewing tobacco juice. "Who hasn't heard of you or heard you? You sing pretty dang loud, girl."

"Yes," says Brooklyn. "I believe you might say the sun comes up just to hear me crow."

"Dang," I say. "You got the part of the rooster, too? Is that you starring in those Kellogg's Corn Flakes commercials?"

"Guilty as charged," says Brooklyn, batting her eyelashes and fanning herself with a hand. "I

took a class at camp about acting in commercials. Those other roosters at the auditions didn't stand a chance."

Before long, Brandon and Michael both jump into our scene. They pretend to be fans who want Brooklyn/Ashley's autograph. I volunteer to snap a photo of the two fanboys with their idol.

"Just back up a piece. Little more. Little more."

They do.

"Don't mind that chandelier dangling over your heads."

They look up.

"I told you I was the Phantom of the Grand Ole Opry! Mwah-ha-ha-ha!"

I mime like I'm cutting a rope.

Brooklyn shrieks first. The two guys follow along. They shift into super slo-mo and shout, "Nooooooo."

Then they mime getting conked on the heads by a crashing chandelier, like the one that plummets down and almost clobbers the audience at Broadway's *Phantom of the Opera*. They all make slow-motion disaster movie moves. They topple to the floor.

When they're a crumpled heap, I say, "Dang. Y'all look more squished than grapes and gooey gourd guts."

"And scene!" calls Brandon.

The three victims of the Phantom's chandelier pop up. We all laugh and applaud one another.

"Okay," I say, "that was fun. Way more fun than following Ashley around stage with my spotlight."

"We should start a comedy improv group!" says Brandon.

"Yes!" I say. Because that's the first rule of improv. You say yes to whatever your scene partners set up and then you move the scene forward. Ms. O'Mara taught us that when we did *You're a Good Man, Charlie Brown*.

"We could call ourselves Spontaneous Combustion," suggests Brooklyn. "We could spontaneously make up scenes and songs from audience suggestions!"

"Yes!" I say again, because that's the rule. "And we'd feature Michael in all the songs."

"With improvised dances for Brooklyn!" adds Michael.

"We could improvise a whole musical comedy from audience suggestions!" says Brandon, who sounds like he's had some prior experience doing improv comedy, too.

"And, with a little rehearsal," says Michael, pulling a wadded-up piece of paper out of his trash bin, "we can perform Thursday night at this open mic night at the Beef 'n' Boards Dinner Theater."

He smooths out the crinkled flyer.

The headline is inviting all Camp Footlighters to

SWING BY THE BEEF 'N' BOARDS DINNER THEATER OPEN MIC NIGHT AND STRUT YOUR STUFF!

A subhead adds, OR YOU CAN JUST CHEER ON FOOTLIGHTS' OWN ASHLEY JONES.

"I trashed this earlier," says Michael. "Because, okay, *Ashley Jones.* She already has her open mic. It's called THIS WHOLE CAMP!"

"This open mic night is at that dinner theater?" says Brandon, crinkling his nose. "The one where Mr. Beasley is the artistic director?"

"But it won't be camp," I say. "So he can't tell us what we can or cannot do. I think. I mean, okay, he *is* the artistic director."

"But it's an *open* mic night," says Brooklyn. "They have to open that stage to anybody. Even us!"

"But a dinner theater?" says Brandon.

"You don't have to eat the prime rib," I tell him. "You just have to jump up in front of the audience and help us create something wonderful, right away."

"Oh," says Brandon. "When you put it that way."

So the next day, after the *Footlights Revue* rehearsal, we hold our own rehearsal.

We work out a format for an improvised musical.

How to open it. How to close it. We block out a rhyme scheme for its big musical number. We have a blast cracking one another up.

Now all we need are a few suggestions from the audience to spark the scene. And a ride to the dinner theater.

We need one of those, too.

Fortunately, the camp bus will be going. Because Mr. Beasley wants Ashley to have a big audience when she wows everybody at the open mic night.

He has no idea we're going to go on, too!

CHAPTER 38

Thursday night at the dinner theater, Ashley goes on first.

Of course.

She also wonders why I'm not up in the booth, operating her follow spot.

"Um, sorry," I say. "It's a dinner theater. They don't have a spotlight. All their extremely hot lamps are busy keeping the prime rib warm at the carving station."

Ashley gives me a look and goes on with, gasp, no spotlight!

She's brilliant, of course. And loud. The pianist

from Camp Footlights is there to accompany her. She sings one of the songs she'll be singing Saturday night at the big *Footlights Revue*, which, by the way, could change its name to *Ashley with Several Exclamation Points*. It's all her, all the time.

She "favors" us with "Tomorrow" from *Annie*.

When she's done, the audience applauds. Politely. The only one truly cheering is Mr. Beasley at the back of the room. Most of the other audience members are making more noise with their clinking silverware than their clapping hands. The dinner theater just served dessert. It's strawberry shortcake. When the waiters spritz on the whipped cream from their spray cans, it sounds like the whole audience is passing gas.

From where we're sitting, it looks like Ashley wants to burst into tears as she, more or less, stomps offstage after her song. Real-world audiences can be tougher than the ones where everybody knows you're the camp director's favorite so they better give you a standing ovation every time you take the stage. Especially if they're enjoying a delicious fruity dessert.

Some other kids from camp perform. So do a few townies—locals who live close to Camp Footlights. We're up at the end of the open mic show.

Spontaneous Combustion takes the stage, and we improvise a ten-minute Broadway musical based on two audience suggestions.

"What's your favorite dessert?"

"Who's your favorite comic-book superhero?"

And, yes, that's how *Mister Softee Meets Iron Man* is born.

The audience loves it. And Michael, playing the heroic Iron Man, sings the heck out of an improvised number about rusty teeth and squeaky knees. Brandon is brilliant as Mister Softee. Especially when he meets his Frosty the Snowman demise on the first day of spring.

The audience loves us.

I know we did great when I see Ashley shooting daggers at us the whole bus ride back to camp.

The next morning, I am summoned to the camp director's office.

This is it, I think. *Mr. Beasley has finally figured out that Ashley isn't his only star!*

He's going to work Spontaneous Combustion into the running order of tomorrow's big, all-camp show. Sure, I'll run the follow spot for Ashley during all her musical numbers. But she can run it for me and my funny friends when we take the stage to wow another audience with our improvised antics!

I, of course, am totally wrong.

To paraphrase Shakespeare, Mr. Beasley is there to bury us, not to praise us.

"The sort of foolishness promulgated by you and your misguided friends at Beef 'n' Boards is not what Camp Footlights is all about, Miss Hart," he tells me. "We're serious about training tomorrow's theatrical professionals today. If you ever embarrass us like that again, you will be asked to leave camp before the end of your term. Things have changed since your benefactor, Ms. Sherron, was a camper. And I will not let you and your merry band of jokesters ruin all that I have strived to build during my brief tenure here!"

So, yeah.

Come tomorrow night, I'll be up in the rafters with my Super Trouper spotlight.

I won't be anywhere near the stage.

I won't be doing anything funny.

I'll just be following Ashley, making sure everybody can see her be brilliant.

CHAPTER 39

Later that Friday morning after the open mic night at Beef 'n' Boards, none of us are happy campers.

Michael is feeling the crush of the upcoming show's deadline.

He has to finish four more costumes for Ashley.

"She needs to be everybody from the Phantom of the Opera to Little Orphan Annie," he says.

I, of course, want to keep our improv comedy troupe going.

When we all have lunch together, I make my pitch.

"We could head to the city on Sunday. Become buskers. I used to do that down the Jersey shore. You do a little show. People toss spare change into your hat or cardboard box or whatever you have. Robin Williams did improv comedy on the steps of the Metropolitan Museum of Art when he was a student at Juilliard."

Michael says he'll be too exhausted on Sunday to do anything except sleep.

"I'm going to be pulling an all-nighter tonight. There are so many seams to be sewn!"

Brandon says he'll be burned out on Sunday, too. "Turns out, the head usher has to fold and staple all the programs. I'll also be pulling an all-nighter."

Brooklyn's another no-go. "We won't have any time to rehearse or work up new structures," she says with a sad sigh. "Madame Lamond is really working us hard."

Unfortunately, I won't have any time to practice with Spontaneous Combustion, either. First, I have to rehearse my follow spot moves with Ashley. Again. To make it halfway interesting, I imagine I'm a prison guard in a movie and I have to swing my searchlight to stop Ashley from escaping. When rehearsal wraps around three p.m., Mr. Skaggs, the stage manager, gives me a new assignment.

"We need a dog," he says. "To play Sandy for the *Annie* number."

"A dog?" I say. "I have a dog at home, but—"

Mr. Skaggs shakes his head. "We need the dog back here and trained for the seven p.m. final dress rehearsal."

"Seriously?" I say.

"Rebecca will drive you over to the nearby rescue group. They're going to let us borrow a dog. It'll be good publicity for their adoption efforts."

Rebecca? I'm thinking. Who's that?

Mr. Skaggs gestures to Echo. Riiiiight. Her real name is Rebecca something-or-other.

"Find a dog," says Mr. Skaggs. "One who looks like Sandy from the funny pages. Train the mutt enough so it'll sit onstage while Ashley sings 'Tomorrow.' Go. Now."

So, yeah. I'm not just the follow spot operator. I'm the chief dog wrangler on the props crew.

It's a very quiet car ride to the animal shelter. Rebecca doesn't have much to say unless Mr. Beasley says it first.

"Nice car," I say.

"Car nice," she echoes back.

And that's the end of our conversation.

We make it to the shelter without her rattletrap car falling apart.

There are so many great dogs, I want to adopt them all. But I find one with shaggy hair and a sweet face that looks like Sandy in the *Little Orphan Annie* comic strip. I'm actually pretty jazzed about working with the dog. After all, I helped train Sandfleas when we adopted her.

The rescue dog and I practice our "sit" and "stay" commands in the open field outside the barn theater. I snatched some chicken from the cafeteria for training treats. The dog is fantastic. Very cute and an extremely quick learner. I go ahead and call him Sandy, just to make things less confusing.

During a break in dance rehearsals, Brooklyn comes out to help me.

"Oh, wow!" She gives Sandy a hug. Sandy gives Brooklyn a good face-licking.

I think Sandy loves Brooklyn even more than he loves me, which is fine. I already have Sandfleas waiting for me at home. I think it's cool that Sandy and Brooklyn get along so well.

A little after seven, Mr. Skaggs comes out of the theater.

"We're ready to work the dog into the number," he says.

"Come on, Sandy," says Brooklyn. I let her lead the dog into the theater. Hey, I don't mind sharing "animal trainer" billing with my roomie.

We tell Sandy to sit and stay at center stage.

Ashley comes out, dressed in her red-and-white Little Orphan Annie costume.

"What's this?" she says when she sees Sandy.

"Your dog!" I say, beaming. I'm pretty proud of how I totally nailed my dog-finding assignment.

Sandy swishes his tail across the stage floor. He's happy to be out of his cage and with humans.

Ashley spins around, looking for someone to yell at. When she can't find anybody, she focuses her fury on me.

"Is this some kind of joke?" she says. "I am allergic to dogs. Where's the stuffed dog we used last year? We always do this number with a stuffed dog."

"B-b-but..." I stammer.

Brooklyn goes to the whimpering Sandy and gives him a hug. He's trembling, because dogs pick up the negative energy when somebody is as angry as Ashley is right now.

"Wait a second," says Mr. Skaggs, coming onstage. "Mr. Beasley told me to have Jacky find a dog for this number...."

"No," says Mr. Beasley, joining him. There is a smirk on his face. He is carrying a giant stuffed animal. It's Clifford the Big Red Dog. They give a lot of those away at the booths on the boardwalk back home in Seaside Heights. "I said have Jacky find *the* dog. As in, she needed to go through the props storage area and find this dog."

"B-b-but..." I'm still stammering. Barely able to utter one word.

"Get this mangy mongrel out of here," Mr. Beasley says, pointing at Sandy. "Take him back to wherever you found him."

"No," says Brooklyn. The way she says it? Mr. Beasley knows she won't back down.

"Well, we can't have him onstage. Didn't you hear? Our star is allergic."

Brooklyn clips a leash onto Sandy's collar. "He can stay with Jacky and me. We'll take care of him."

Mr. Beasley's eye twitches. I get the feeling (and not for the first time) that he is slightly afraid of my roommate. I also get the feeling that he was trying to set me up with the whole "find a dog" run. I think he wants me to quit Camp Footlights. He doesn't want to have to tell Latoya Sherron he kicked out her scholarship student.

"Fine," he says. "Suit yourself. Just kindly remove your dog from my stage!"

"Come on, Sandy," says Brooklyn.

I make a move to go with her and the dog.

"Miss Hart?" says Mr. Beasley.

"Y-y-yes, sir?"

"Where do you think you're going? This is our final dress rehearsal. You need to be upstairs on that catwalk, operating your follow spot."

I just nod. I'm afraid if I speak, I'll start stuttering, and I really don't want to give Mr. Beasley or Ashley the satisfaction of doing that to me!

So I dutifully head to the back of the auditorium, where there's a ladder that leads up to my follow spot booth. Brooklyn comes along with Sandy.

When we're alone together at the rear of the house, I can tell: Brooklyn's "Brooklyn" has been fully activated.

"Mr. Beasley is a bad, bad man," she whispers. "We need to bring him down, Jacky! Big-time."

CHAPTER 40

Brooklyn and I love having Sandy share our room. Brooklyn has fallen hard for the dog. She heads into town, finds a pet store, and makes sure our new roomie has food, dog bowls, toys—everything.

"I talked to my mom," she tells me first thing Saturday morning. "We're going to officially adopt Sandy and take him home with us when camp ends next weekend."

Wow, I think. *She's right.*

Not about her mom and the dog. Of course she's right about that. Duh. I mean she's right about camp coming to an end!

This is my second Saturday. I have only one more week at Camp Footlights. And I can't believe I'm spending my second showcase opportunity running a Super Trouper follow spot for Ashley Jones.

I like being *on* the stage, not shining a lighthouse beacon down at it.

Next weekend, I promise myself, I'm going to do something spectacular. Maybe land a big part, even if I have to beat out Ashley for the role. Okay. That would be impossible. Mr. Beasley is always the final judge and jury. But maybe there will be a fun part that Ashley won't want. Yeah. Impossible again. She wants them all.

But I have to do *something* next Saturday night.

I promise myself that my last shot on the Camp Footlights stage will be my best shot.

This Saturday, however, I climb the ladder, put on my headset, and make sure my follow spot is ready to glow. The audience files in below me. I wait for my first cue.

It comes right after the overture. (It's prerecorded on a cassette tape; there's no orchestra at Camp Footlights.)

Ashley is waiting in the dark in front of the act curtain.

"And go follow spot," Mr. Skaggs tells me over the headset.

I flip open my shutter and spotlight the star of the night. My hot white light sparkles all over her sequined costume. Ashley starts belting. Michael told me that's what you call it when a singer uses her "high chest voice" (I'm not sure I have one of those).

"Ethel Merman started doing it in *Girl Crazy*," Michael explained. "That was way back in 1930."

Yes, like a lot of theater kids, Michael knows his Broadway legends and lore.

Tonight, Ashley's belting out "Don't Rain on My Parade" from *Funny Girl*. When the show was on Broadway, Barbra Streisand sang this song. Ashley is bellowing it so loudly (it's borderline yodeling), Ms. Streisand might be able to hear her out in Hollywood.

"...Life's candy and the sun's a ball of butter."

Interesting lyrics. I'm guessing this song is a big hit at the local dinner theater. They have warm rolls and tiny plastic tubs of soft butter.

Next comes the big hook that gives the song its title, "Don't Rain on My Parade."

Just when I'm wishing there were thunderstorms in the area because, come on, I've already had to sit through two whole weeks of Ashley's parade, there is a commotion in the wings of the stage.

It's Sandy! The dog.

I can make out his silhouette as his claws *tick-tick-tick* across the wooden floor. Soon, he reaches center stage and is sharing the spotlight with Ashley.

Ashley gives him a look and a quick *shoo* gesture with her free hand. Her other hand is busy doing dramatic stuff like being clenched into a fist and waving away imaginary rain clouds.

Sandy doesn't take the hint. Instead, he leaps up into Ashley's arms.

Reflexes overriding her brain, Ashley catches him.

The crowd goes, "Aaaaaawww." They love it.

CHAPTER 41

On the next verse, allergic Ashley starts sneezing. That startles Sandy.

So he leaps out of her arms and scampers stage left.

Now *my* reflexes and audience-pleasing instincts kick in. The crowd loves the dog. So I follow *him* with my spotlight instead of Ashley. The audience applauds. They think this is a funny bit. That Sandy's antics are just part of the "Don't Rain on My Parade" opening number. Maybe they're expecting him to raise a rear leg at the big finish and, you know, "rain" on the red velvet curtain.

Ashley, like a trained moth, accompanies the bright light of the follow spot, which I'm focusing on Sandy. When Ashley leaps back into its circle, she shoots me such a dirty look, I decide to narrow my beam on Sandy's face.

So Ashley bends down to share that tiny halo of white with him.

That earns us more laughs.

I narrow the beam even further, turning it into a bouncing white tennis ball that I send sailing left. Sandy chases after it. Ashley (still singing between sneezes) races after the dog and her diminished spotlight.

The audience is roaring with laughter. Yes, girls, somehow your mother found a way to be funny without even being onstage. I swing the light to the right; Ashley and Sandy run after it. I tilt it up the curtain; Sandy and Ashley take turns hopping up into my beam.

"Jacky?"

I finally hear Mr. Skaggs's voice in my headset.

"Jacky?!?"

I think he's been hollering my name ever since I decided to improvise my little light show.

"Stay with Ashley! Stay with Ashley."

I sigh and do as I am told. I widen out the circle just as Brooklyn dashes onstage to grab Sandy.

Soon, there is a new voice coming over my headset. "Miss Hart?"

It's Mr. Beasley.

"Climb down from your post immediately. You

and Brooklyn are to return to the main lodge and wait for me in my office!"

Sooooo...

I guess Ashley will do the rest of the revue without a follow spot.

I also guess I'm in pretty big trouble.

CHAPTER 42

Brooklyn, Sandy, and I exit the barn theater and trudge across the open field toward the main Camp Footlights lodge.

It's only a little after eight, so the sun is just starting to set. Behind us, we hear Ashley belting out another show tune. She can no longer bask in the glow of the spotlight, but the audience is showering her with applause.

"Sorry about that," says Brooklyn.

"About what?"

"Letting Sandy run loose onstage. I kind of accidentally on purpose dropped his leash. That, of course, was after I also accidentally on purpose brought him backstage in the first place."

I shrug. "Hey, I didn't have to follow him with my spotlight."

Brooklyn smiles. "Or turn the spotlight into a glowing ball for him to chase."

"I figured it was more entertaining than watching Ashley sneeze-sing her way through the Streisand song."

"You figured correctly. I guess I shouldn't've brought Sandy to the show." Her voice drops into a whisper. "But, sometimes, it's like I have this little devil sitting on my shoulder, egging me on to do mean and nasty stuff. But only to mean and nasty people."

"I have one of those devils, too," I whisper back eagerly. "Mine is a little less particular in the egging department. She'll make me do all sorts of wacky stuff."

"Like eat all that boardwalk food before you rode all those boardwalk rides?"

"Exactly. My little devil was very chatty that day."

We take Sandy up to our room and then head down the hall to the camp director's office, where, of course, we have to wait. Mr. Beasley won't be there until the curtain goes down on *The Footlights Revue*.

"I'm sorry you won't get to dance tonight," I say

when I realize that Brooklyn's been, basically, cut from the show.

"It was my choice," she says. "Or, the devil on my shoulder's choice. Either way, I went along for the ride. I'm just so tired of everything up here being about Ashley, Ashley, Ashley."

"Who else should it be about?"

Mr. Beasley has stepped into his office.

"Ashley Jones is a once-in-a-generation talent." He takes a seat behind the big wooden desk. Brooklyn and I are sitting on the other side, in short visitor chairs. It's like we're at the kiddie table for Thanksgiving dinner.

"I'm the one who let the dog run across the stage," Brooklyn tells him.

Mr. Beasley glares at her. Until his left eye starts twitching. And then his left nostril. His whole face is a herky-jerky, twitchy mess.

"I consider the dog's arrival onstage to be an accident preceded by a bad choice," Mr. Beasley tells Brooklyn. "It was a mistake to bring the dog to the theater after we had specifically cut him from the *Annie* number. But I'm sure you didn't realize it could be dangerous for Ashley. And while I don't approve,

I understand your motivation, Brooklyn. The original Broadway show was done with a real dog. You were only hoping that our rendition of the song could meet those same high standards. Unfortunately, our Annie is allergic to pet dander."

And, just like that, Brooklyn is off the hook. In fact, Mr. Beasley is almost applauding her initiative and dedication to making the show the best it could possibly be.

Brooklyn gives me a *What the what?* sideways glance. I shrug. Once again, I get the feeling that, for whatever reason, Brooklyn terrifies Mr. Beasley.

I, on the other hand, do not.

And I'm his next target.

CHAPTER 43

Which brings me to you, Miss Hart," says Mr. Beasley, his smile broadening. "You were derelict in your duty to the show! Worse, you sabotaged a fellow performer while she was onstage."

"No, sir," I say. "I just didn't want her allergies to get in the way of—"

He slams his fists down on the desk. Pens rattle in cups.

"I do not care what you wanted, Miss Hart. I only care about what the show and its fabulous star need."

"B-b-but A-A-Ashley w-w-was sn-sn-sneezing."

"Heavens," says Mr. Beasley with a look of disgust as I start stammering. "Who is your voice and diction coach here at camp? Whoever they are, I should fire them!"

"I-I-I d-d-don't t-t-take..."

Brooklyn jumps in to rescue me. "We don't take voice and diction classes," she says. "Not up here, anyhow."

"Yes," says Mr. Beasley, still glaring at me. "That much is obvious. Miss Hart? I know that for whatever misguided reason, our legendary alum, Latoya Sherron, thought enough of your talent to get you a spot and pay your camp fees for this summer's final session. However, I plan on calling her to tell her what you did tonight. How you violated every sacred show business tradition. When she learns of your misbehavior, I feel quite certain that she will withdraw her scholarship posthaste."

I take a deep breath. Try to slow my heart rate.

I'm calling up all the tips and tricks Ms. O'Mara has taught me about how to not stutter when I'm feeling stressed or flummoxed.

Somehow, I find my voice. It comes out steady, slow, and strong.

"You don't have to call Ms. Sherron, Mr. Beasley."

"Oh, yes I do. She'll want to know that she's been wasting her money."

"You don't have to call her," I say, "because I'm quitting. Maybe you can give her a refund for the last week."

Mr. Beasley sniffs a little. "We don't really do refunds...."

"Wait, Jacky," says Brooklyn. "You can't quit."

"Yes, I can. I don't belong here, Brooklyn. I never did. I never will."

Mr. Beasley folds his hands over his belly and

leans back contentedly in his squeaky wooden chair. He looks so happy. Victory is his. I have given him exactly what he was hoping for.

"Would you like to use my phone to arrange transportation home?" he asks.

"Yes, sir."

Mr. Beasley gestures grandly to the clunky avocado-green handset sitting on his desk. "Kindly limit your call to three minutes. Long-distance charges are astronomical."

He waits and watches while I dial home. Rotary phones made the whole long-distance-call thing take so long. You had to dial one. Then the three-digit area code. Then the seven-number phone number. There was no such thing as speed dial. You had to stick your finger in a plastic hole, turn the wheel, and wait for it to rotate back to the start, ELEVEN DIFFERENT TIMES!

Dad answers on the second ring and wonders what's wrong.

"Things just aren't working out up here," I tell him. "I don't fit in."

"Well," he says, "I guess it's good you learned

that now. You don't want to waste your life chasing a dream you can't catch."

That stings. Until I realize that Dad's probably remembering his days playing minor-league baseball for the Oneonta Yankees. And the injury that stopped him from chasing the dream he couldn't catch, even though he was very good with his glove.

We move on and work out the details. Someone will pick me up tomorrow morning.

I'm going home. For me, summer camp is over.

"But, Jacky?" says Dad.

"Yeah?"

"No matter what new thing you end up doing with your life, you'll always be a shining star to me."

That makes me feel a little better.

Not much. But a little.

CHAPTER 44

First thing Sunday morning, I'm standing in front of the lodge with my suitcase.

Brandon, Michael, Brooklyn, and Sandy are there to see me off. They all look sad. Sandy has his tail tucked between his legs. I guess I sort of do, too.

"Don't go," says Brandon. "If you leave, Mr. Beasley wins. And he's just a gray sprinkle on our rainbow cupcake."

Michael shakes his head. "They're trying to do to you what they did to me."

"I know," I tell him. "And it's working."

Brooklyn is about to say something, but I see our dusty family van crunching up the gravel driveway.

"That's my ride," I tell my friends. "It was great meeting you guys. I gotta go."

"No," says Brooklyn. "You don't have to."

"Uh, yeah I do. My sister just drove, like, two and a half hours on the Garden State Parkway to pick me up. I look forward to seeing all the great things you three are gonna do. And, Michael?"

"Yeah?"

"Sing every chance you get!"

"Jacky's right," says Brandon. "'Sing out, Louise!' That's a line from *Gypsy*."

"We know," say Brooklyn and Michael, because, ta-da, they're theater kids. Me? I did not catch the reference. I take it as further proof that I'll be better off back home, doing typical middle school stuff, like...I don't know. I've never really been typical. Guess there's a first time for everything.

My big sister Sydney, who's on a short break from her summer classes at Princeton, volunteered to drive up to fetch me.

"So," she says as we drive away from Camp Footlights, "remember that time when I thought I'd ruined my life because I did poorly on that one test?"

I nod. How could I forget? My big sister surprised us all by coming home. Then she surprised us some more by bawling her eyes out and sobbing herself to sleep.

"Remember how you told me it was just a bump in the road?"

"Yeah," I say. "And you said it was more like a pothole."

"Right. And then you told me that we can fix potholes. You just need to pour in hot asphalt. Sure, you said, it's stinky and pothole repairs always back up traffic and people honk their horns and shout, 'Get out of the street, lady!' You told me to shout back, 'Sorry, can't right now. Need to smooth out this bump in my road.'"

"Wait a second," I say. "You remember all that? How can you? As I recall, you were falling asleep at the time."

"Only because you were telling me that silly story, Jacky. You have a gift, little sister. You know how to make other people laugh and smile and feel better."

"Ha," I say, sinking down in my seat and putting my

sneakers up on the dashboard. "Tell it to Mr. Beasley."

"No thanks. I'd rather tell it to you. And I'll also remind you that this is not the end of the world. It's a bump in the road. Or a pothole."

I shake my head. "No, Sydney. This is a 'Bridge Out Ahead' in the road. My way forward has been completely washed away by a Noah-sized flood. I have no choice but to turn around, take a detour, and find another route through life."

"Or," says Sydney, "you could rent a boat."

"Then what would I do with my car? I mean, that's how I was on the road. Even though I don't have a driver's license."

Sydney smiles. "It's a ferryboat. It'll take you and your car. Like the Staten Island Ferry."

"Will I get to see the Statue of Liberty?" I say, because making up a new silly story with my big sister suddenly feels better than feeling sorry for myself, which is what I've been doing ever since Mr. Beasley ordered me to climb down from my spotlight perch.

We riff on the ferryboat for a few miles.

Then, even though neither one of us can really sing like Michael or Ashley, we sing along to Bryan Adams on the radio.

I don't tell Sydney to "Sing out, Louise."

Because, for one thing, that's not her name.

For another, I'm ready to leave all that showbiz, theater kid stuff behind.

If you don't belong to the club, you really shouldn't use their secret phrases.

CHAPTER 45

That afternoon, back home in Seaside Heights, everything looks the same, but it feels different.

It even smells different. All those delicious aromas of greasy food wafting up and down the boardwalk? They don't smell so delicious anymore. Okay, that might have more to do with my most recent barf-a-thon than my mood. But still. You ever sniff cold French fries? They never smell as fantastic as the hot and crispy ones.

I'm on my bike, which I used to call Le Bike because I wanted to be one of zose French girls in ze movies, riding around with ze wicker basket filled with ze fresh-cut flowers and ze long, crusty loaf of bread. Then I called it La Bicicletta because I was feeling more Italian and imagined my one-speed two-wheeler was actually a Vespa motor scooter.

Now I just call my bike "my bike" because I've decided it's time to move on and drain all the goofy, whimsical, fanciful junk out of my life—the way you can drain all the color out of a TV show just by twisting a knob to the left.

The ocean is still the ocean, the boardwalk is still the boardwalk, but I feel out of place. Like, even though I've been gone for only two weeks, this isn't my home anymore. Like I'm the one thing that isn't the same as it used to be.

Except, of course, there's my old booth. It is definitely not the same as it was two weeks ago.

You might recall how my old Balloon Race with the water pistols and the open-mouthed clown heads was about to become the Smack 'Em! Whack 'Em! arcade where you can blast all sorts of bad guys with semiautomatic squirt rifles.

That happened. Plus, the new owner, that guy named Anthony, hired a new barker. Someone to take my place.

And, of course, it's my old nemesis since kindergarten—Ringworm. He's still showing off his Mohawk hairdo and heavy-metal air guitar talents while snarling at the world. My clever rhymes are ancient history. Ringworm has his own brand of snappy patter.

"Blast 'em, splash 'em, whack 'em—in the face, dudes! Or are you too chicken, bruh? Bruck-bruck-bruck."

I lower my head and pedal away fast so Ringworm won't notice me spying on my old place of employment.

When I get home, I cruise around the block. Several times. I really don't want to go into the house. If I do, I'll have to explain to Emma, Riley, Hannah, Victoria, Sophia, and Mom why I quit camp. Dad and Sydney already know the gist of the story.

I didn't fit in.

I'm not cut out for showbiz.

Everybody else, especially Sophia and Victoria, will want to hear all the juicy details.

At least, that's what I'm thinking when I make my third loop around the block and past our front stoop.

Emma, the Little Boss, is on the top step with her hands on her hips. "Jacky? Will you puh-leeze quit riding around in circles?"

I coast to a stop.

My sisters come tumbling out the front door.

"There you are!" gushes Hannah, with her hands over her heart. "We were all so worried about you!"

"You need to get in this house right now!" commands Victoria. "Immediately."

"Ms. O'Mara is here," says Sophia. "She needs to talk to you. Then I need to talk to you about that boy named Michael. The hottie with the hair swoosh?"

"They fired Mr. Beasley!" shouts Riley.

What?

Riley shouts again: "Who's Mr. Beasley?"

Ms. O'Mara comes out onto the porch. "Jacky? Don't unpack your bags." ·

"Ha!" says Victoria. "Jacky never unpacks until, like, two weeks after any family vacation. It's so annoying."

"Good," says Ms. O'Mara. "Throw your stuff in my trunk, Jacky. I'm driving you back to Camp Footlights. Now!"

CHAPTER 46

T hey fired Mr. Beasley?" I say when we're cruising north on the Garden State Parkway.

By the way, traveling back and forth like this, between New York and New Jersey, I'm getting super-familiar with all the rest stops and attractions along the way. (One of these days, I want to stop at the Cheesequake Rest Area at milepost 124. I imagine their cheeseburgers are incredible—what with all that cheese sliding around after the cheesequake.)

"The board of directors took a vote," Ms. O'Mara tells me. "It was unanimous. They were not happy campers when they heard how Mr. Beasley has been running things this summer. Someone told Latoya

that Mr. Beasley was shutting down a lot of very talented kids just so he could spotlight one camper."

"Ashley," I say. "With an exclamation point."

Ms. O'Mara nods. Don't forget—she came to that first showcase. She's seen Ashley in action. And I definitely know about Mr. Beasley spotlighting her because I was the one running the spotlight.

"Of course," Ms. O'Mara continues, "that Ashley is extremely talented. A true triple threat. But that doesn't mean everyone else's whole summer should revolve around her."

"That was kind of Mr. Beasley's plan," I say.

"Well, Latoya's on the board. So is that movie star Caroline Jean Risvold. There are also some Broadway producers, theater professors—all sorts of heavy hitters. When they heard how Mr. Beasley was running the place, they took a vote. Camp Footlights is supposed to be there for all the campers, not just the teacher's pet."

"So Mr. Beasley's really gone? They fired him with only one week left in the session?"

"Everybody wishes they would've known about this sooner. How he treated you—well, that was the straw that broke the camel's back."

"Poor camel," I say. "Maybe we should find him a chiropractor. Or a back brace that would fit over his hump. And, by the way, why was he hauling straws? Did the soda fountains in the desert run out?"

Ms. O'Mara laughs and shakes her head. "You were seriously going to quit being funny, Jacky?"

I shrug. "I was going to try. I thought maybe I could become an accountant. Would I need to do math to be an accountant?"

"Uh, yeah."

"Okay. Cross that career off the list. So where did Mr. Beasley go?"

"Not far. Latoya tells me he's still the artistic director at a dinner theater close to the camp."

"Beef 'n' Boards. Our improv troupe performed there, and, yes, I taught everybody what you taught me."

That makes Ms. O'Mara smile. "Each one teach one."

"So who's running the camp for the next seven days?" I ask.

"A recent theater arts grad named Rebecca Griswold will handle things through next Sunday."

"Who's Rebecca Griswold?"

"Latoya says she was Mr. Beasley's assistant."

"Oh. Riiiiight. Rebecca. Never knew her last name."

She's talking about Echo. The flunky who took me dog-scouting even though she probably knew the show didn't actually need a real dog. They just needed a big red stuffed Clifford from the prop closet.

I figure Echo can handle Camp Footlights for a

week. She just needs to repeat stuff she heard Mr. Beasley say all summer long and she's golden.

"And of course there's the big show this Saturday night," Ms. O'Mara tells me as we cross the New York state line.

"There's a big show *every* Saturday," I remind her.

"True. But this is the biggest of the big, the most important one of them all. This Saturday is closing night. The grand finale. Henry Hendricks will be in the audience."

"Who's he?"

"Only the most important talent agent in all of New York City. So, Jacky?"

"Yes?"

"I have only one question for you."

"The answer is yes. I do floss on a regular basis."

"Good. But are you ready to show Camp Footlights and the world who you truly are? Are you ready to let them see the real Jacky Hart?"

"I will if they'll let me."

"Don't worry about them, Jacky. *You* just need to do *you!*"

CHAPTER 47

Ms. O'Mara drops me off in front of the main lodge.

"Ms. Griswold requested that you see her before you move back into your room," she tells me.

Who? I almost say. Then I remember: Ms. Griswold is Echo. I need to come up with some way to remember that. Maybe, in my head, I'll call her Ms. Griswold-wold-wold. Give the name an echo of its own.

"Will you be coming in with me?" I ask with elevated eyebrows, which is my way of letting Ms. O'Mara know that I sure would like it if she'd be my wingperson on this mission.

"Nope," she says with a happy smile. "Part of showing the world who you are is doing it all on your own."

"Even if people are mean to you?"

"Especially if they're mean to you."

"O-kay. See you later?"

"Definitely. Next Saturday. Latoya and I want to see you shine in front of Henry Hendricks."

She helps me unload my suitcase, and then, zoom, she takes off.

None of my camp friends are there to greet me. Maybe they've been told to stay in their rooms until after my audience with the new, interim camp director.

So I grab my bag and trudge up the steps to the main lodge.

"Ms. Rebecca Griswold" is written on a piece of cut tape pasted over Mr. Beasley's plastic nameplate. I knock on the door.

"You may enter," she calls out—much louder and clearer than back when she was Mr. Beasley's assistant.

"Uh, hi," I say, stepping into the office and throwing my arms open wide like I'm making an entrance in a musical. "I'm baaaaaack!" I give it a good *Poltergeist* spin, because I'm all about doing movie catchphrases whenever possible.

"Yes," says Ms. Griswold. "So I see. Ms. Sherron and Caroline Jean Risvold will be so, so pleased. This was their idea. Not mine."

O-kay. The words are her own. The sneer? Pure Beasley.

"Miss Hart," she continues, "as your new, temporary, non-permanent, and provisional camp director, I'd like to give you a word of advice. Something I learned while I was earning my master of fine arts degree. Ashley Jones is a star. She might be difficult and a diva, but stars often are."

Not Latoya Sherron, I want to say. *She's kind and generous.*

But I don't say anything because it's clear the new acting (and I use that term loosely) camp director wants to hear only herself speak. In fact, I think Echo is trying to earn a new nickname: Monologue.

So she blah-blah-blahs and yadda-yadda-yaddas for five full minutes.

Finally, she tells me that I'm "welcome to participate in next Saturday's showcase."

"The one that Henry Hendricks is coming to?" I say.

Ms. Griswold looks surprised. "Oh. You heard about that? All the way down in New Jersey?"

"No. Ms. O'Mara just told me on the ride back to camp. She's my drama club advisor. She's also besties with Latoya Sherron. They did *Annie* together on Broadway when they were kids. They had a real dog in their show."

I give Echo a look—just so she knows I know she knew that our dog-scouting excursion was a wild goose chase, even though dogs were involved instead of geese.

"This Saturday's showcase will be a talent show," the temporary camp director informs me. "You may perform solo or in a group. For instance, if you want to dance, please dance."

Echo lets that hang there. Okay. Fine. She knows that, when it comes to dancing, I have two left feet, which, by the way, would make it very difficult to go shoe shopping.

"Gotcha," I say, straightening up, hoping I'm dismissed.

"One last thing," she says. "At this Saturday's showcase, there will be absolutely no improvisation. This is a theater camp. Theater is a dramatic celebration of the written word, be it those of William Shakespeare or Gilbert and Sullivan. Therefore, all material must be scripted, not made up on the fly."

"Fine," I tell her.

Because I know that a lot of the most famous improvisational companies, like Second City in Chicago, take their best improvised bits and polish them into written sketches. Maybe we'll do that.

When I'm (finally) free to leave Ms. Griswold's office, Brooklyn, Michael, and Brandon are waiting for me in the hall.

"We heard a rumor that you were back," says Brooklyn with a grin.

"Yeah," I say. "I just needed to run down to the Jersey Shore this morning, walk my dog, and then come back up here. Speaking of dogs, where's Sandy?"

"My mom took him home."

"Your mom was here?" says Michael. "How come you didn't introduce us?"

"Because Brooklyn was embarrassed to be seen with us," quips Brandon. "And can you blame her? I know I can't."

Brooklyn laughs. "Mom was in a hurry. She had to go to a 'very important, early-morning meeting.'"

"On a Sunday?" says Michael, arching a skeptical eyebrow.

"What can I say?" Brooklyn shrugs. "Mom's a busy, high-powered woman."

"Those are my favorite kind," I say. "So who wants to do something fun and funny for next Saturday's showcase?"

"What're you thinking?" asks Brandon.

"A skit," I say. "Something I write that shows off Michael's singing, Brooklyn's dancing, and your wickedly dark wit."

"What will you be showing off?" asks Michael.

"I dunno. Maybe just me."

CHAPTER 48

My friends and I spend the rest of the week going to classes (which, by the way, are soooo much better now that Mr. Beasley's gone) and working on our sketch comedy scene.

We're all super-nervous and excited about Henry Hendricks, the big-shot talent agent, seeing us perform in the closing-night showcase. We have butterflies in our stomachs, and not just from singing outdoors in the woods near a butterfly bush.

I write us a pretty funny bit that'll be simple to stage. All we need is a café table and two chairs. Brandon and I will play a snooty couple out to dinner at a fancy New York City restaurant where everybody on the staff wants to be in show business. It's kind of a funny take on how all the waiters in New York City are really wannabe performers of some sort. Michael will be our singing waiter; Brooklyn our dancing server. In the skit's final twist, we reveal that, in this particular restaurant, even the paying customers (Brandon and me) are wannabe actors. Or in Brandon's case, a wannabe juggler. (It's one of the special skills listed on his resume.)

The bit's pretty hysterical, if I do say so myself, which, hello, I just did.

A couple of campers watch us rehearse it. So do some of the staff. They all agree. We're funny. We're also having a blast working on it together.

Ashley Jones, of course, does not drop by any of our rehearsals. In fact, we don't see her around camp at all very much during the week. I imagine that she's moping in her "star of the summer" cabin, pining for the good old days when Mr. Beasley turned Camp Footlights into Camp Ashley with an Exclamation Point.

But she will be in the Saturday showcase. In fact, when Ms. Griswold passes around the running order, it shows "Ashley Jones!" going on right after *Restaurant Revue*, which is the title we came up with for our piece.

Before we know it, it's Saturday.

We've had a tech rehearsal and our dress rehearsals.

Now, finally, we have our audience.

The dressing room is buzzing. The smell of pancake makeup and hair spray is in the air.

I peek through the act curtain and see Ms. O'Mara and Ms. Sherron in the middle of the auditorium. I might see Henry Hendricks, too. I can't be sure. I have no idea what he looks like.

Ms. Griswold gives our audience a little speech to start the show.

"Another closing," she says, "another show. We've all learned so much this summer here at Camp Footlights. We've made new friends. And lost others."

She drops her eyes. I think she's observing a moment of silence for Mr. Beasley.

The audience squirms in their seats and someone coughs. I'm guessing they've all heard why the former camp director was given the heave-ho. They're not really interested in honoring him with any sort of moment-of-silence tribute.

Finally, Ms. Griswold makes a grand gesture to the red velvet drapes behind her.

"Curtain up!" she proclaims. "It's showtime!"

Five amazing acts go on before us. There's singing, dancing, dramatic readings.

But not many laughs. We hope to fix that.

Brooklyn, Brandon, and I are waiting in the wings. Ready to go on right after the guys doing the sword fight from *Romeo and Juliet*. Not the scene or the words. Just the sword fight.

As the swords thunk, Michael joins us.

"Weird," he says.

"What?" I whisper.

"Ashley. Her costume isn't in the dressing room. Neither is she."

"She's probably just outside," suggests Brooklyn. "Warming up her voice. Doing some breathing exercises."

"Maybe," says Michael. "But usually she's in her chair doing hair and makeup until it's time to make her first entrance."

Onstage, the Shakespeare sword swingers fake-stab one another, clutch their fake wounds, and topple to the floor, moaning and groaning in their dramatic fake deaths.

Blackout!

"Forget Ashley, you guys," says Brandon. "We're on!"

CHAPTER 49

As the audience applauds, the swashbucklers grab their gear and scramble offstage in the darkness.

That's our cue to push our props into place. A few seconds after we're settled into position, the lights come up.

Yes.

Brandon and I are framed by the hot white circle of my trusty Super Trouper spotlight, which somebody else is running for our sketch.

I'm super-nervous. My family isn't in the audience (they could only make that long trip to Camp Footlights for the first Saturday showcase), but I know Henry Hendricks is. More important, I know

Ms. O'Mara and Ms. Sherron—my biggest support-
ers and boosters, the two women who believed in me
before I believed in myself—are out there. I want to
make them proud!

"I hear everybody on the staff at this restaurant
really wants to be in show business," I say to Brandon
as we both slice prop food on our plates.

"Really?" says Brandon in a snooty, lockjaw voice.
"In New York City? What a surprise."

This earns a knowing laugh from the audience.

Michael makes his entrance as the singing waiter.

"How are you finding everything?" He trills the
standard waiter question operatically.

"With our eyes and, unfortunately, our noses,"
says Brandon. "This fish has gone bad!"

Brooklyn swirls in, making her jazzy, leaping
entrance.

She scoops up the rubber fish off Brandon's plate
with one hand and spanks it with the other.

"Bad fish!" she scolds the prop. "Bad, bad, bad,
bad, bad!"

The audience is doubled over with laughter as she
twirls offstage.

"Oh, waitperson?" I say to Michael. "What's this fly doing in my soup?"

Michael leans in to examine my soup bowl. "I would give you the classic answer and say 'the back-stroke,' but that looks more like water aerobics."

More laughs.

"Perhaps we can bring you something else?" says Michael with a very stiff bow.

"Fine," huffs Brandon. "I'll just have a cheese-burger, no onions."

"Right," says Michael, jotting a note on his order pad. "Extra onions."

"I said no onions!"

"Right, sir. Double onions."

"I don't want any onions at all!"

"Very good. I'll make sure you have them all. And would you like a little wine with your meal?"

"Oh," I say. "A little wine would be marvelous."

Brooklyn leaps back onstage and does a few acro-batic toe twirls, then she and Michael start to whine very annoyingly.

"Mwaaaaah," they cry. "You two don't liiiiiiike our fish or our onions! Waaaaa."

"Well," says Brandon, "what do you suggest we eat?"

Michael snaps out of the whine. He gestures to the sound operator up in the booth. "Hit it, maestro."

A karaoke track from the classic Broadway musi-cal *South Pacific* comes thumping out of a pair of speakers onstage. Michael starts singing. He's mag-nificent and funny all at the same time.

"We've got shrimp, we've got beef.
We've got chicken out our ears.
We've got beets and stinky cheese that no one's
ordered in years.
We've got crepe suzettes, crab croquettes, all sorts
of fancy food.
What ain't we got?
Food that's goo-d."

The audience applauds! So do Brandon and I, in character.

"Are you an actor?" I ask innocently, batting my eyelashes.

"Shouldn't you be starring in a musical comedy on Broadway?" asks Brandon.

"Why, yes," says Michael modestly. "However could you tell?"

"Because I'm an actor, too!" I say, springing up out of my seat, grabbing a roll from the bread basket, and launching into a parody of a famous Shakespeare soliloquy. "Alas, poor dinner roll. I knew him, Horatio."

Michael gasps. "How'd you know my name is Horatio?"

I shrug. "It's on your name tag."

Now Brooklyn comes back onstage. She's ball-room dancing with a coatrack.

"I wanted to work in the coat check room," she says. "But I couldn't get the hang of it."

While she Ginger Rogers her way across the stage with her wooden partner, Brandon grabs three dinner rolls and starts juggling them.

"I love New York!" he shouts. "When you go out to eat at a nice restaurant, everybody is in show business! Even the customers!"

And we end by singing our own wacky version of "There's No Business Like Show Business." We add a line—"*Except, maybe, the restaurant business!*"

The audience loves it!

We have to take two curtain calls.

Even though the follow spot is blinding us all, I can make out Ms. O'Mara and Ms. Sherron.

They're both on their feet and finger-whistling like they're trying to hail a cab.

"Wow!" Brooklyn whispers to me as we take yet another bow. "I'm so glad Henry Hendricks decided to come this weekend!"

"Me too!" I say along with Michael and Brandon.

But as soon as we're backstage, we learn the sad truth from Echo.

"Mr. Hendricks never picked up his ticket."

CHAPTER 50

I cannot believe he went to the Beef 'n' Boards Dinner Theater instead of coming to see my first show as interim, part-time, temporary camp director!" says Ms. Griswold. "Mr. Beasley did this to me! He's trying to make this the worst one-week job of my life!"

She's so upset, I have a feeling she'll never echo her old boss again. She stomps away, biting her fist so she won't burst into tears.

"That's probably where Ashley went!" says Michael, putting two and two together. "Mr. Beasley gave Henry Hendricks the wrong address so the only talent he'd be seeing tonight would be Ashley!"

The Camp Footlights talent show is taking its fifteen-minute intermission early because the final number of the first act, Ashley, didn't show. She's up the road entertaining the prime-rib-and-roasted-potato crowd. Latoya Sherron and Ms. O'Mara come bustling backstage to tell us how great we did.

"Thanks," says Brandon, sounding so sad, you'd think somebody had just squished his s'mores in the dirt to make the marshmallows crunchier.

"Yeah," says Brooklyn, sounding equally bummed.

"I'm glad you two saw it," I say, trying to silver-line the dark cloud of gloom hovering over all our heads.

"You guys?" says Ms. O'Mara. "What's wrong?"

"Yeah," says Ms. Sherron. "Typically, when someone comes backstage to tell you how good you were, you say, 'Gee, thanks,' and get all giddy."

"Ashley and Mr. Beasley win again," says Michael with a sigh.

Ms. Sherron is confused. "What do you mean?"

"They hijacked our talent scout," he tells her. "Henry Hendricks is over at the Beef 'n' Boards Dinner Theater, where Mr. Beasley is the artistic director."

"And we use that term loosely," says Brandon.

"I remember Beef 'n' Boards," says Ms. Sherron. "It was here when I was a camper, too." She turns to Ms. O'Mara. "Good thing the rental company didn't have that Mustang convertible I reserved."

"Huh?" I say.

Ms. O'Mara smiles. "All they had left was a big, boxy van."

"With plenty of room for all four of you kids," says Ms. Sherron. "Come on."

"Um, where are we going?" I ask.

"Over to Beef 'n' Boards. We're taking this show on the road!"

We tell Ms. Griswold where we're going.

"Good," she says. "And if you see Mr. Beasley, tell him I hope he breaks a leg. Literally!"

Nobody says much during the five-minute van ride from Camp Footlights to the dinner theater.

I think we're all too busy fuming and vowing revenge.

"Kids?" says Ms. Sherron, looking up at us in the rearview mirror. "Don't be so glum. Just try to remember what the great Muhammad Ali said. 'You

don't lose if you get knocked down. You lose if you *stay* down.'"

"So," says Ms. O'Mara, turning around in the front passenger seat, "it's time to get up. You four have another show to do. A repeat performance of *Restaurant Revue.*"

"At the dinner theater?" I say.

Ms. O'Mara nods. "Yep. Because that's where Henry Hendricks is."

Brandon raises his hand to ask a question.

"Yes?" says Ms. O'Mara.

"How are we going to even get onstage? Mr. Beasley won't invite us to perform."

"And," says Brooklyn, "it isn't open mic night."

Behind the wheel, Ms. Sherron smiles. "Kids? Leave getting onstage to me."

CHAPTER 51

Ms. Sherron slips the Beef 'n' Boards box office person her platinum card.

We're in.

The six of us make our way into the dimly lit dinner theater. The whole place reeks of beef grease and canned green beans. Up on the thrust stage, Ashley is sparkling in the lights. She's in another of Michael's sequin-studded gowns. She smiles down at a bald guy seated at a front-row table, buttering his dinner roll. I'm guessing that's Henry Hendricks. Mr. Beasley is seated right beside him. He's beaming.

"For my next number," Ashley says, her voice very husky and breathy, "I'd like to favor you with a little something from my most recent one-woman show,

Ashley with an Exclamation Point. It's a number I wrote—the lyrics and the music. I call it 'My Best Friend Is Me.'"

"Find a seat, guys," whispers Ms. Sherron. "We're gonna make our move right after Ashley takes her final bows." She turns to Ms. O'Mara. "Come on, Kathy. We need to hit the ladies' room. Bring your makeup bag."

Five, maybe ten minutes later, Ashley finally wraps things up by belting "There's No Business Like Show Business." She's practically shouting it down at the first row. Poor Mr. Hendricks. He may need to take a shower to clean up after the spittle spritz Ashley just gave him.

When Mr. Beasley clicks the stop button on his boom box and her musical accompaniment ends, Ashley blows the audience (aka Mr. Hendricks) a kiss.

"Thank you all for coming out tonight," she gushes. "Thank you for making tonight so super-duper special! Next stop? Broadway!"

The dinner theater crowd applauds. Politely. I also hear a lot of forks clinking plates. They just served dessert. Chocolate cake with a raspberry on top.

Ashley makes her grand exit stage left just as Ms. Sherron, looking stunning in a simple dress and cardigan, enters from stage right. She sparkles when she steps into the lights, and her shimmering has nothing to do with sequins or glitter powder.

"Hiya, folks!" she says, and waves to the crowd.

The audience gasps.

They can't believe how lucky they are! *Did Grammy and Tony Award–winning superstar Latoya Sherron just step onstage at the Beef 'n' Boards Dinner Theater?*

Oh, yes, she did.

"Wasn't Ashley terrific?" says Ms. Sherron, doing a fingers-to-palm pitter-pat of a clap to the wings. "That girl's going places. You know, she sort of reminds me of me. When I was young and so full of hope and dreams. All I really wanted to do was make it to Broadway...and maybe Forty-Second Street."

Suddenly, Ms. Sherron launches into the song "42nd Street."

The crowd goes wild. She's doing it a cappella, of course, because Mr. Beasley brought boom box cassette tapes only for Ashley's numbers. Plus, the former camp director looks so shocked, with his eyes popping out, I don't think he could push a button if his life depended on it. His tablemate, Mr. Hendricks, is smiling from ear to ear, wowed by the awesomeness that is Latoya Sherron.

When she finishes the line about *"Come and meet those dancing feet, on the avenue I'm taking you to..."* Ms. Sherron suddenly stops.

"Hold on, folks. Wait a second. Why am I just singing about dancing feet when I have a marvelous dancer here with me tonight?"

The audience gasps again. They turn in their seats, hoping to catch a glimpse of some other Broadway superstar who just happened to drop in at Beef 'n' Boards tonight.

"In fact," Ms. Sherron continues, "I think this young woman is the finest dancer in all of New York. Of course, I'm a little biased." She gestures toward the audience. Toward our table way at the back. "Because my daughter, Brooklyn Sherron, is here with us this evening."

"What the what?" say Brandon and Michael.

I'm sitting there with my jaw hanging open like I'm a ventriloquist's dummy without a ventriloquist.

Brooklyn is Latoya Sherron's daughter?!?

"Could you get me another autograph?" whispers Michael.

Brooklyn winks at him. "Maybe."

Then she gives me a funny *Whoops, sorry* shrug. Like maybe she forgot to mention SOMETHING super-important?!?

"Ladies and gentlemen?" Ms. Sherron says onstage. "I think with a little encouragement, Brooklyn just might come on up here and make this a mommy-daughter number!"

The audience cheers and whistles and chants, "Brook-lyn, Brook-lyn!"

Brooklyn slides out of her seat and scampers up the aisle to the stage.

"Hang on, Mom," she shouts. "I'm comin'!"

The audience laughs and cheers. Brandon and Michael turn to each other.

"Did you know?"

"No, did you?"

"Nope."

I start realizing stuff I should've realized sooner. Last Sunday, when Ms. O'Mara drove me back to camp, Brooklyn's mom came up to Camp Footlights but couldn't stay because she had to go to a very important meeting—the board meeting about firing Mr. Beasley.

And that's why Mr. Beasley always seemed slightly afraid of Brooklyn. He knew who her mother was, even though Michael, Brandon, and I didn't. This might also explain why Brooklyn didn't want to come with us when we all bused down to the city to see Ms. Sherron's Broadway show and why Brooklyn never tells anybody her last name.

Wow.

I snap out of my thoughts long enough to take in the show. The mother-daughter number is fantastic.

Latoya Sherron sings while Brooklyn Sherron does the incredible choreography. (How she tap-dances in tennis shoes, I'll never know.) Then, as a bit of an encore, Ms. Sherron slides into singing "The Lullaby of Broadway," and Brooklyn improvises some amazing moves and steps. Madame Lamond would be proud.

♪ ♫ *Come and meet my daughter's dancing feet, on the avenue I'm taking you to...* ♫

When they finish, the whole crowd (except Mr. Beasley) gives the duo a standing ovation. Henry Hendricks is applauding louder than anyone. He's also shouting, "Brava! Brava!"

And me?

I'm clapping until my hands hurt, but my jaw is still hanging open.

Brooklyn is Latoya Sherron's daughter?!?

CHAPTER 52

Why didn't you tell us?" I whisper when Brooklyn scampers back to our table.

(Her mom is still onstage, doing a number from *Birds of a Feather*, the Broadway show all of us except Brooklyn saw down in the city.)

Brooklyn shrugs. "Hey, you were the girl who did a Shakespeare show with a famous Broadway superstar this summer, but you never even told anybody at camp about it because you wanted to show them that you were something special—just by yourself."

"True."

"Well, I've lived with *Latoya Sherron* my whole life. And I'm me, Jacky. Not Latoya Sherron's daughter. I insisted that she not tell anybody at camp that we're related. I want people to judge me for who I am and what I do, not by what my mother's done."

I nod. Because, yeah. It kind of makes sense.

"You guys?" says Brandon. "Get ready. I think she's about to introduce us."

"Thank you, thank you," says Ms. Sherron up onstage. "You're too kind. But how about we keep this show going? My daughter, Brooklyn, isn't just an incredible dancer. She's pretty darn funny, too. Especially when she's sharing the stage with her friends. Ladies and gentlemen, put your hands together for Brooklyn, Brandon, Michael, and Jacky. It's time for their *Restaurant Revue!*"

Ms. O'Mara helps us grab a pair of chairs and our table. We carry it all to the stage.

As we're setting up, I notice that Mr. Beasley has his head in his hands.

Because Henry Hendricks is sitting up like somebody who just had a delicious cup of coffee right after a long nap. I don't mean to say that he slept through most of Ashley's musical stylings, but...

Anyway, girls, to make a long story a little shorter, we're a hit.

A smash hit.

All the jokes land. We get more laughs at the dinner theater than we did back at Camp Footlights. Michael's singing is fantastic. Brooklyn's dancing is amazing. Brandon and I are pretty funny, too.

We also get a standing ovation when we take our bows.

There's **no show** business like business I **know**, except, maybe, the restaurant business!

And, of course, Mr. Beasley isn't joining in with everybody else.

In fact, he's gone.

He must've left when he knew we'd wowed the crowd. (That "bad fish" slapping bit works every time.)

When the houselights come up, we shake hands with the audience.

"You kids are amazing!" says one guy with Russian dressing on his shirt. "Amazing."

I eavesdrop on Ms. Sherron's conversation with Michael.

"I meant to tell you back at camp," she says. "You have an incredible voice, Michael. Incredible. If you don't mind, I'd like to tell my vocal coach about you. And my agent. And the producers of *Birds of a Feather*. We need an understudy for the part of Joey."

Michael's eyes get a little moist. Somebody has seen him for who he is, not what other people tell him he can be. And that somebody is, hello, LATOYA SHERRON!

In a surprise twist, we discover that Madame Lamond was in the dinner theater audience!

"Monsieur Beasley requested my assistance with Ashley," she says, crinkling her nose disdainfully. "But, I am afraid, there is only so much one can teach to one who thinks they already know all there is to know. However, you, Brooklyn? Mwah! *Tu étais incroyable, ma belle amie!*"

I think she told Brooklyn she was incredible.

Now Henry Hendricks comes up to me.

"Katherine O'Mara tells me you're Jacky Hart."

"Yes, sir."

"And you wrote that sketch?"

"Yes, sir."

"How old are you?"

"Almost thirteen."

He reaches into his suit and finds a business card. "Keep it up, kid. And, in just over five years, when you turn eighteen, give me a call."

I take the business card.

"Hello, Mr. Hendricks!" Ashley has come into the auditorium. I can tell by the raccoon circles of smeared mascara under her eyes that she's been crying.

For the first time since I met her, I feel sorry for Ashley Jones.

She's just like the rest of us. A scared kid who

wonders if she'll ever have what it takes to make it in show business.

"Isn't Ashley fantastic?" I say to Mr. Hendricks. "I'm sure you could tell from her show—she's a triple threat. She can sing, dance, and act. Me? I'm what they call a single threat. I make people laugh. Or run away. That's what they do if I sing or dance...."

Mr. Hendricks laughs and shakes his head. He reaches into that suit pocket again and pulls out another business card. He hands this one to Ashley.

"Give me a call. You'd be terrific in commercials. And there are all sorts of touring musicals." Believe it or not, he nods toward me. "With a recommendation like that from Jacky Hart, I'm willing to give you a shot, kid."

Brandon leaves with a business card, too.

In fact, that impromptu talent show at Beef 'n' Boards more or less launched five different careers. So, you see, Grace and Tina, doing scary stuff, like crashing a dinner theater's show, can sometimes lead to all sorts of what Madame Lamond might call "incroyable" stuff.

Brandon Maloney went on to become a fantastic stand-up comedian.

Ashley Jones was cast, almost immediately, in a tooth-whitening commercial (the first of many) and went on to star in a soap opera where she's had amnesia several times.

And, of course, you guys know what happened to Michael because you met him last year when we went backstage after seeing *Les Misérables*. Plus, we have all his albums.

And that hot crush I might've had on him? It chilled before summer turned to autumn.

Of course you also know that Brooklyn Sherron now choreographs for the Alvin Ailey American Dance Theater in New York and that she and I still get together on a regular basis.

And me?

Well, two weeks after my eighteenth birthday, Henry Hendricks helped me land a spot in the writers' room for *Saturday Night Live*. Yes, girls, I started out as a writer before I became a performer on the show.

So, Grace and Tina, I want you to have a great summer this year, like I did way back in 1991—even though I didn't know I was having such a wonderful time until after it was almost done.

I know you two are both about to do things that might scare you.

But those scary things might also take you places you never thought you could go.

So, come on. Step outside your comfort zone. Take a few risks.

But, please, promise me one thing: You'll never climb a Ferris wheel to howl at the moon.

It's dangerous, and besides, it's already been done. That was me being me.

You two just need to do you.

For his prodigious imagination and championship of literacy in America, **JAMES PATTERSON** was awarded the 2019 National Humanities Medal, and he has also received the Literarian Award for Outstanding Service to the American Literary Community from the National Book Foundation. He holds the Guinness World Record for the most #1 *New York Times* bestsellers, including *Max Einstein*, *Middle School*, *I Funny*, and *Jacky Ha-Ha*, and his books have sold more than 400 million copies worldwide. A tireless champion of the power of books and reading, Patterson created a children's book imprint, JIMMY Patterson, whose mission is simple: "We want every kid who finishes a JIMMY book to say, 'PLEASE GIVE ME ANOTHER BOOK.'" He has donated more than three million books to students and soldiers and funds over four hundred Teacher and Writer Education Scholarships at twenty-one colleges and universities. He also supports forty thousand school libraries and has donated millions of dollars to independent bookstores. Patterson invests proceeds from the sales of JIMMY Patterson Books in pro-reading initiatives.

CHRIS GRABENSTEIN is a *New York Times* bestselling author who has collaborated with James Patterson on the I Funny, Jacky Ha-Ha, Treasure Hunters, Katt vs. Dogg, and House of Robots series, as well as *Word of Mouse, Pottymouth and Stoopid, Laugh Out Loud,* and *Daniel X: Armageddon.* He lives in New York City.

KERASCOËT is the pen name of Sébastien Cosset and Marie Pommepuy, a couple of French graphic novel authors and illustrators living and working in Paris.

Join the most spine-tingling, creepy-crawling, giggle-producing kid's detective club ever. That's *ever*.

TURN THE PAGE TO GET STARTED!

prologue

ADULTS JUST LOVE ASKING US WHAT WE WANT TO BE when we grow up. I guess they think it's cute when we answer, "an astronaut," or "a rock star," or "your boss, so I can make you stop asking me questions."

But it's hard to predict the future. I never even thought about saying I wanted to be a detective, any more than a grass inspector or a night watchman at a mattress store. I don't mean those are bad jobs, or that they aren't interesting in their own ways—they're just jobs I never even thought about.

But that was before the murders in my building. That's right—*murderS*, with a capital *S*. Not one, not two, but...well, keep reading. You'll find out who died, who almost died, and whose lives I helped save.

(Hint: One of them was my own.)

I'm not even the only kid at school who's a detective now. But we don't let just anybody join our club. Our members have to be curious, creative, and good at spotting clues. Does that sound like anyone you know?

Does that sound like...you?

chapter 1

At the marble-topped chess table in the wood-paneled lounge of our apartment building, I sat across from my elderly neighbor, Kermit Herman-son. Both of us were playing fast and furiously. I wanted to win so badly it was killing me.

It was my turn, so I moved my knight into the center of the board and stopped my chess clock with a CLICK—starting Kermit's time. We each had only ten minutes to play the whole game.

Kermit raised an eyebrow and stroked his long gray beard. "Are you sure you vant to do zat?" he asked. His accent made him sound like a mad doctor from a monster movie. He's told me he's from

Sweden, and I've never met anyone else from Sweden or whose English sounds like his.

"I've never been so sure of anything in my life," I told him. "Why, are you getting nervous?"

Kermit was hard to beat, so I figured a little trash talking couldn't hurt.

Even though Kermit taught me how to play chess when I was six years old, these days, we rarely played face to face. I usually made my moves on my way to and from school, and he usually made his moves as he came and went from his daily walks around our Chicago neighborhood. But today was Sunday, so when we met each other in the elevator, we'd decided to grab some snacks and sit down for a game.

"Vell, eet ees your funeral," said Kermit, raising one eyebrow.

He smiled and moved his bishop to block me. CLICK.

I had opened with a series of aggressive moves called the Fried Liver Attack. (I know it sounds crazy but look it up: It's real.) Usually I play defense, because Kermit is a much better player. But this time I wanted to throw him off his game by going on the offense—and his latest move showed me it was actually working.

I attacked again. CLICK.

"I wouldn't call the undertaker yet," I told him.

"You are off to impressive start," admitted Kermit. He had been moving quickly and confidently, but now he was hesitating. "I only hope you know how to checkmate."

"Oh, I know how to checkmate, all right. The only question is how many moves it will take me."

He picked up his queen and then put it back down in the same place. He tugged at his shirt collar like it suddenly felt too tight.

I smelled victory—a victory that would be all the sweeter because I would be there to see the look on his face.

Beads of sweat broke out on Kermit's wrinkly peach-colored forehead. He moved again and stopped his clock again—CLICK—trying to block me with a pawn. But he was only delaying the inevitable. Suddenly, it was like I could see three moves ahead. I knew exactly what I needed to do to steer him toward the endgame.

"Are you sure you want to do that?" I asked, teasing him.

"Maybe not," he admitted. "I am not feelink like myself today."

"Or maybe you've just forgotten what it feels like to lose."

CLICK.

Kermit sipped his tea, which smelled like liquid campfire smoke. He'd already eaten all of his lemon cake except the crumbs.

"Zat ees possible," he said. "Or maybe…"

He frowned.

"Maybe what?" I asked.

It seemed like he was thinking about resigning. In chess, when one player knows they have no way to come back and win, they quit the game by tipping over their queen. It's a super dramatic way to say, *Fine, I give up—you win!*

Well, Kermit gave up, all right. But he didn't tip over his queen.

Instead, he rolled his eyes, knocked the pieces onto the floor—and collapsed onto the chessboard.

MIDDLE SCHOOL

- ○ *The Worst Years of My Life*
- ○ *Get Me Out of Here!*
- ○ *Big Fat Liar*
- ○ *How I Survived Bullies, Broccoli, and Snake Hill*
- ○ *Ultimate Showdown*
- ○ *Save Rafe!*
- ○ *Just My Rotten Luck*
- ○ *Dog's Best Friend*
- ○ *Escape to Australia*
- ○ *From Hero to Zero*
- ○ *Born to Rock*
- ○ *Master of Disaster*
- ○ *Field Trip Fiasco*
- ○ *It's a Zoo in Here!*
- ○ *Winter Blunderland*

TREASURE HUNTERS

- ○ *Treasure Hunters*
- ○ *Danger Down the Nile*
- ○ *Secret of the Forbidden City*
- ○ *Peril at the Top of the World*
- ○ *Quest for the City of Gold*
- ○ *All-American Adventure*
- ○ *The Plunder Down Under*
- ○ *The Ultimate Quest*
- ○ *The Greatest Treasure Hunt*

MIDDLE GRADE FICTION

- ○ *Becoming Muhammad Ali* (cowritten with Kwame Alexander)
- ○ *Best Nerds Forever*
- ○ *Laugh Out Loud*
- ○ *Minerva Keen's Detective Club*
- ○ *Not So Normal Norbert*
- ○ *Pottymouth and Stoopid*
- ○ *Public School Superhero*
- ○ *Scaredy Cat*
- ○ *Unbelievably Boring Bart*
- ○ *Word of Mouse*

MAX EINSTEIN

- ○ *The Genius Experiment*
- ○ *Rebels with a Cause*
- ○ *Max Einstein Saves the Future*
- ○ *World Champions!*

For exclusives, trailers, and more about the books, visit Kids.JamesPatterson.com.